BRUTAL CAPTURE

LEE SAVINO

TABITHA BLACK

ONE

Haley

I'M HAVING the strangest dream. I'm lying on a dewy lawn, with moisture seeping into my skin from below. A fern leaf brushes my face. It's nighttime but the sky is bright with the light of the full moon. No—*five* moons. Five? What the fuck?

I run a hand over my head and my fingers get snagged. My hair is tangled from sleep. Something bites my bare thigh sharply, and I swat it, but miss. Some sort of lightning bug zooms away—but it's bigger and more wicked-looking than any insect I've ever seen before. And it was bright red, unlike any lightning bug I've ever seen.

I rub my leg. Whatever it was, that thing bit me, and it hurt. Which sucks, but what sucks even more is what the sharp pinch didn't do.

It didn't wake me up. I'm already awake. This isn't a dream. This is happening to me.

Where am I?

I sit up, my damp limbs aching, trying to get my bearings. I'm wearing a transparent negligee, my nipples and

1

areolas on display through the filmy white fabric. There's a relentless pounding in my skull, and a bitter taste in my mouth. My lips are cracked, and when I rub them, I taste blood. I'd kill for something cold to drink.

A branch cracks, and I whirl around, my heart hammering in my chest. A ghostly shape pushes its way through the brush, and staggers to a stop next to me. The figure hunches over, hands on knees to catch its breath.

"Ulf," exclaims a high-pitched voice. The newcomer's wearing a pale, flimsy-looking robe that brushes the tops of her thighs. And nothing else. The robe is pretty see-through, like the one I'm wearing.

The woman pushes back her long hair to gape at me. Her eyes are a bit too big for her face. And her ears... have pointed tips. Like an elf's.

Maybe I'm at some sort of costume party... and I drank too much? That would explain my woozy head. But that wouldn't explain why she doesn't sound like she's speaking English—or any language I've ever heard.

"Um," I manage. My lips feel too big for my face.

Before I can ask where I am and what I'm doing here, the woman leans in, her huge eyes wide.

"What are you doing?" she hisses. "You can't stay here! The Alphas are coming! We must run!" Reaching down, she grabs my hand, wraps long, slender fingers around my wrist, and yanks me to my feet, nearly dislocating my shoulder. She's a lot stronger than she looks. She tows me behind her and we go crashing into the undergrowth.

She's tall, too, with at least a foot on me, and even though it's nighttime, there's something unusual about her. Her skin shimmers in the moonlight, looking... green.

I follow her, trying to match her long-legged strides, branches and leaves whipping my face, my chest, my legs.

"What's happening?" I say between pants. My words sound garbled to my own ears. Everything feels wrong.

"The Alphas are coming. We must run."

She said this before but it means no more to me than it did the last time. "The who?"

"The Alphas! This way..." Reaching back, she grabs my wrist again and tugs me through a prickly bush, shushing me when the leaves scratch me and I squeal.

Once we're through the bush, she stops and lets go of my wrist. We're in a tiny alcove, surrounded by dense foliage. She narrows her eyes, assessing me from head to toe. "Who are you?" she says. The sounds she makes when she speaks don't sound like English at all, but the garbled syllables somehow make sense.

"Who are you?" I repeat.

"Sian." The tips of her pointed ears twitch.

"My name is..." I rub my head with chilled fingers. Why can't I remember my own name? What the fuck is going on? "Haley," I manage. "Please tell me where we are. Why are we running away? Why are we out here in the middle of the night?" We've gone too far into the forest for this to be a party. Maybe I've gotten into geo-caching? In my sleep?

Her eyes narrow. "You don't know?"

"I don't know!" I wipe my mouth, fighting back the wave of panic which has been threatening to crash over me ever since I opened my eyes to find myself in this bizarre nightmare.

"It's the Hunt of the Moons," she says, as if speaking to a small child. "Where the Alphas hunt for Betas."

"Betas?" I repeat dumbly.

"The Alphas used to hunt Omegas, but now there are none left. Well, almost none. But we maintained the tradition here on Arboron."

"Arboron?" I squawk like a parrot.

3

"The Forest Kingdom."

"Forest Kingdom." Sounds like something from Dungeons and Dragons. "Is this like a Ren Faire, with some sort of fantasy theme?"

"A what?" Sian's ears twitch again. She's gone all out with her elf costume.

I swallow, wincing when the skin on my lips cracks. "Do you have anything to drink?"

Sian looks around for a moment, then glides over to a nearby branch and plucks something round off it. She punches a hole in the top by sliding her thumb in, and raises it to her lips. She takes a sip before handing it to me.

I mimic her movements, upending the thing—which is about the size of a grapefruit—and letting the sweet liquid slide down my raspy throat. It's unlike anything I've ever tasted before but it's so damn good. "Thank you," I tell her after I've sucked the thing dry.

She regards me. "Where are you from?"

It's a good question. Where *am* I from? Trying to recall anything from my past is like trying to wade through toffee. I have small bits of memory but so much is hazy. I know my name is Haley... and I'm not from around *here*. "Um..."

"No matter. We have to keep moving or they'll catch us. We don't want to be caught this soon."

"We don't?"

"The best Alphas prefer a challenge." Moonlight limns the curve of her lips. She bounces her eyebrows at me.

"Wait," I rub my forehead. "Do you *want* to be caught?"

"Of course. That's the best part of the hunt. But we don't want to be caught right away. Follow me." She spins on her heel and sets off again, and I scramble to follow her. My thighs are trembling, and pain blazes in my bare feet when I skid over some moss-covered rocks. Sian dashes down an unseen path, her dark hair rippling like a flag

4

behind her. She never slips or bangs into a bush. I follow like a baby elephant, ping ponging between tree trunks and smashing into thick clumps of glow-in-the-dark ferns. The fronds are neon orange.

"Holy hell." The organizers of this Forest Kingdom event thought up some insane decor. I catch the tip of a frond between my fingers. Feels real.

"Shhh," Sian hushes me.

"I'm trying," I huff back. "I'm not used to running at night." Or running at all.

Sian reaches back and pulls me onward before I can tell her I don't want to be caught by an Alpha. I have a ton of other questions I want to ask, but the most pressing is: what happens if an Alpha catches us?

Maybe I don't want to know.

After what feels like hours of running, we push our way through another thick bush and emerge near a huge waterfall.

I stop, panting for breath, bending over in a vain attempt to soothe the stitch in my side. Whoever I am, I don't run marathons for fun.

"Haley, we must keep going." There's an urgent note in Sian's voice but it's been there since she first stumbled across me, and now I'm ready to revolt. I've banged into too many thorn bushes and stubbed my toes against too many logs. My throat is screaming for water or more of those juicy fruit things. I need to figure out how the event organizers changed the sky to show not one, not two, but five full moons.

What the hell sort of Ren Faire is this?

"I can't," I gasp, clutching my side. The initial rush of adrenaline I got when we first set off has subsided, and now all I want to do is lie down. "Just give me a second."

With a sigh, Sian seats herself on the edge of a boulder.

A bright red lightning bug zooms into my face and I rear back. "Geez. This is like a bad trip. I swear I'm never doing 'shrooms again."

Sian chuckles. "You speak funny."

"You know, I was going to say the same thing about you."

A harsh screech rings out. It's high above us in a towering tree, but we both jump. "My god," I say, pressing a shaking hand to my chest. "That sounded like a ptero-dactyl." It didn't sound like a fake Jurassic Park sound effect either. It sounded real. "You said we're in the Forest King-dom? What state are we in?"

"State? This is a Kingdom."

"Right," I say. Sian isn't going to break character. She's obviously a method actor, hired by some insane Fantasy Faire organizer who's intent on making all his Tolkien dreams come true.

"Okay. Fine. Try telling that to the IRS," I mutter to myself.

Sian jumps up. "We need to go. The river dilutes our scent, but soon the Alphas will be close enough to scent us."

"And that's bad, right?"

"If they scent us, they can find us." She sounds like she's explaining things to a total noob. "We don't want to be found until the end of the hunt."

"Why not? What will they do?" Unless her answer is that we'll be killed and eaten, I'm not running another foot.

"They'll—" Her ears twitch. She cranes her head around. "Do you hear that?"

I strain for a moment, listening. The forest is full of sounds—creaking insects, leaves rustling in the treetops, the distant squawking of the pterodactyl bird.

Sian holds up a finger. "The hunters."

There's a rhythmic thudding, like hoofbeats. And it's

getting louder. "You're kidding me," I say. "They're on horseback? While we're on foot? That's so unfair!"

"Tyrlee," Sian says, and glances around, obviously trying to decide where to go next.

"What?"

A blast of a horn rings out, louder than a pterodactyl cry. There's a distant sound of whooping and cheering. *The hunters.*

"Come on!" Sian leaps onto a rock in the middle of the river and splashes to the opposite bank.

Frozen to the spot, I stare after her until she's disappeared into the foliage, the pounding of the hooves getting louder until it's echoing in my aching skull.

Well, fuck.

TWO

The Hunter King

AT NIGHT, the forest tells its secrets. The trees breathe every time the wind rustles their leaves. Night birds call from their secluded nests. Insects sing. The grasses whisper back.

A breeze gusts through the shivering trees, carrying a potent perfume. I lean back and sniff the air. My chest and arms are bare, but the night is not cold. Nor is it dark. The pale purple glow of the five moons lights my way.

I pull my tyrlee to a stop and pat her neck before leaning back and drawing deep lungfuls of the damp night air. Brokk has ridden up beside me, and there are a few more Alphas behind us, laughing and calling to each other. Their scents rise in a thick haze—the musk of lust.

I'm wearing simple breeches and boots, with a few leather straps to hold my daggers criss-crossing my chest. The other Alphas are wearing armor. One of them is wearing a ceremonial robe.

"Let's place bets on who can find the most Betas," Brokk says. "Can you even run in such ornate armor, Golzon?"

Golzon, a big Alpha with polished weapons, glares at Brokk, and turns back to a cluster of his friends.

"You need to be more like our king," Brokk calls, nodding to me. "Carry little, move lightly. Become one with the forest. The rocks and the trees."

I nudge my tyrlee onward, not wishing to be a part of this conversation. There are too many people in this grove. Too much heat radiating off the tyrlees' heaving bodies. Deeper in the woods, glow bugs float over the bushes, creating a rippling carpet of reddish light. Patches of brilliant orange—the yaknos fern groves—shimmer through the trees.

The forest is my home. Being out here at night, under the light of the moons, in the forest—I am at ease. As the chosen king of Arboron, I have no choice but to spend some time in the palace, but this is where I'm truly free.

Out here, among the trees.

My tyrlee slips away from the crowd, but Brokk keeps pace easily.

"It's time." Brokk pulls out a giant horn from his saddlebag and offers it to me. "Come on. It's your duty, as king, to announce the start of the hunt. It's tradition."

I stare at him. It makes no sense for a hunter to announce himself. A hunter must run silently, without clanking armor or a clumsy sword. He must creep like the smallest forest scuttler, and roll in the mud to hide his scent. He does not stomp or shout, or blow an ulfdamn horn.

Brokk rolls his eyes as if he knows what I'm thinking. "Very well. I know how much you love tradition and your kingly duties. Permission to start the hunt, my king?"

I jerk my head.

Brokk raises the horn to his lips and blows. The sound fills the forest, blasting like the bellow of a dying tyrlee. The birds and insects fall silent. The Alphas whoop and cheer and urge their tyrlees forward, in the direction of the subtle Beta females' scents. The best trackers follow their noses. The worst follow their friends.

Brokk whoops. I lean over my tyrlee and she surges forward, weaving through a copse.

A few tree lengths away, Golzon curses when a branch whips him in the face. He rode right into it. He might as well be blind.

The Alphas are all hunters but the night is mine. We're all hunting for the same thing: pussy.

The Hunt of the Moons. An Arborii tradition for generations, yet these days it is nothing more than lip service to the great before times, when Omegas were still plentiful. Lacking Omega females, we hunt Betas. They have the same anatomy, the same holes, we are able to slake our basest desires on their curvaceous bodies—and yet. And yet.

No slick.

No rut.

No knot.

No claiming bites.

No offspring.

There's a holler behind me and I twist in my seat. One of the Alphas leaps off his tyrlee and rushes toward a cluster of Cex trees, chasing a flash of white. The sweet, pleasing smell of an Ulfarri Beta female tickles my nostrils.

"He's found one," Brokk mutters, pushing his braid back over his shoulder.

I nod. The scent should spur me to ride my tyrlee hard to find a sweet Beta of my own to use. But I lean back and pat my tyrlee's neck instead, hushing her when she grunts in eagerness to move.

I used to love the Hunt of the Moons. But over the past couple of years, it has grown tiresome. Fake. Pointless.

Brokk and I watch the Alpha drag his prize out into the

clearing and push her into the soft grass. The warrior is almost demented with lust—it is apparent in the brusque way he tears the Beta's gown clean in two, exposing her naked, plump body just moments before he plunges himself inside her. Her cries are muffled by his hand over her mouth as he fucks her with ruthless abandon.

Some might say it is savage, but we Ulfarri have always been slaves to lust. Those few remaining elders who have witnessed or even experienced the rut say it is akin to madness, that an Alpha in rut is no longer coherent or able to control even his own body. That is why Omegas in estrus produce so much slick—to ease a frenzied Alpha's passage even without preamble or care. He can rut her to his heart's content with no fear of doing too much damage to her more delicate, feminine body.

Beta females, on the other hand, do not produce slick, but their cunts do get wet when they experience pleasure. Which is why most of the females who take part in the annual hunt have signed up for it. They enjoy being chased and held down. Ulfarri are known as The Brutal Ones.

This extends to the way we fuck.

The Beta female pants, "Yes, yes, yes," in time with the Alpha's thrusts.

Brokk cocks his head as he watches the frenzied coupling happening a few yards away from us. "The hunt's off to a good start."

I shrug. There was a time when this scenario would have made my cock hard, and I would have hastened away to catch a female of my own.

Now, I'm bored.

"Ulf," Brokk exclaims, straightening in his saddle. "I think I saw something. Over there!" He kicks his tyrlee into motion and sets off. I'm about to follow him when I catch the faintest whiff of something delectable. It's so light, I almost missed it. Inhaling deeply, I let out a low growl when I smell it again—slightly stronger now. The tart sweetness of a leeberry, combined with honey, and dewy grass. But there's a deeper, musky scent which goes straight to my groin.

The floral scent makes my canines tingle, and my heart pumps faster.

Pounding hoofbeats make me turn. Several of the Alphas who'd fallen behind are passing me at a gallop. Did they catch the same scent?

I nudge my tyrlee's sides and she lunges forward. I lean over her neck, becoming one with her movements. Being king has some advantages. Taking my pick of the tyrlee is one of them. My mount, therefore, is swifter and stronger than most, and I overtake the other Alphas easily. Once I'm in the lead again, I close my eyes and concentrate, following the scent.

It's getting stronger. The source is near.

I guide my tyrlee, veering down a hidden side path. The glowing ferns part before me. Let the other Alphas gallop on. I don't know what I'm about to find, but I may not want to share it.

My tyrlee is panting, her flanks heaving, so I slide off her and pat her broad neck, making reassuring clucking noises. I set off, padding lightly, my nostrils flaring as I follow that delicious, honeyed aroma.

I know this forest more intimately than anything. It's my home. So I know where I am, even in the gentle lilac glow cast by the moons. I would know it blindfolded.

I'm close to the waterfall.

The scent of my prey is so strong now, I grow dizzy, as if I've drunk too much wine. There's a tightening in my balls and lower belly, and a tingling in the base of my spine. I want to beat my chest and roar, but force myself to continue moving slowly, carefully.

After what feels like several moon-cycles, I come to the edge of the clearing and peek through the dense foliage of a yaknos fern.

That's when I see her.

A strange, tiny female with a cloud of dark hair, and dark eyes shaped like lysia petals. She looks like a ghost, partly from the moonlight, partly because of the translucent wet gown clinging to her curvaceous body, and partly from the luminous light brown color of her skin. She's climbing out of the river. As she steps carefully up the bank, streams of water trickle in rivulets down her heaving chest, her bare legs, her long, thick hair...

I'm transfixed. I've never seen anything lovelier.

Who is she? And why is she emitting this scent that is making me ache?

A tiny voice in the back of my mind is whispering the answer, but my rational side is arguing that it cannot be. *She* cannot be.

Can she?

As she moves closer, I force myself to inch back. I must remain hidden until the last moment. Decades of hunting have made that instinct as natural to me as breathing.

And yet... that scent. I've never smelled anything like it before. But I've heard tales...

Ulf, I'm hard. My cock is painfully rigid, straining against my breeches.

No female has ever had this effect on me before. But then, no Beta I've encountered has ever smelled this way.

Omega, my inner voice—my entire being—insists.

She cannot be. There are no Omegas left on Ulfaria.

There are now, the inner voice reminds me. The Wanderer King found one on his travels, and brought her back to be his *majesta*. There was a Kings' Council. I was there. I saw her: a pink, helpless thing, bundled in Khan's arms, covered in his seed. I could smell her in spite of that. And while the scent was slightly different, that underlying musk which makes my mouth water...

That was the same.

Aurus commanded his mages to find more Omegas, to have them brought here. He took the first one, of course—arrogant fool that he is—and demanded that more be obtained. But surely this little female picking her way across the grass cannot be one of them. She would be too precious. Too valuable. The magicians would have gone to great lengths to bring her here to our planet. They would not go to all that trouble just to let her run free in my forest.

I take a deep, silent breath, and that ulfdamned scent hits me anew. This time, it's like a log to the head. My cock hardens and my musk rises as my body heats, and all my doubt disappears.

This is an Omega.

She is in my forest, on this night. The Hunt of the Moons.

It is a sign.

She is destined to be mine.

I am the Hunter King... and she is my prey.

THREE

Haley

MY SKIN PRICKLES with a sudden chill. There's a bite to the air, and the hoofbeats are getting closer. Some instinct tells me to wade into the water. The waterfall is huge and impressive, crashing down from a great height, then spreading into a gigantic lake, which narrows to a river a little way away. If this is a hunt and the hunters are on horseback, will they have dogs, too? If so, getting into the water will help disguise my scent.

Goddamn Sian, and every actor wannabe who won't break out of character to explain what's going on. Goddamn past me who decided to take part in some crazy Wild Hunt re-enactment. Goddamn the organizers and whoever gave me E or Molly or whatever psychedelic drug that's making me hallucinate Day-Glo orange ferns and whatnot. Once I get out of here, I'm writing a strongly worded review on their webpage.

At least more memories are coming back—random things, like my preferred search engine and seltzer brands. But not anything specific about who I am, or how I got here.

I hobble to the river bank and dip my toe into the dark, murky liquid. The cold knifes up my leg.

I don't want to do this. I want to be somewhere warm and safe, in a bed, surrounded by familiarity and my unicorn stuffies. But the pounding hooves are getting louder and louder—until my fear overcomes my dislike for the cold. Sucking in air, I dive in and start swimming for the other side.

I surface with a burst, with the panicked thought: what if I can't swim? My numbed limbs move as if they had a mind of their own, and I'm across the mini lake in no time. When my feet hit the muddy bank, I'm so cold, it hurts. It's eerily silent as I creep out of the water, wishing I had a nice down jacket. I can't stop shivering. My nipples are like pebbles.

At least the pounding of hooves has died down. Maybe my trick of getting in the water worked somehow.

I hope Sian's okay. She tried to help me. Sorta.

I stagger up the river bank and slip into the shadows by the treeline. I stop and wring out my long, soaked hair with numb hands. My teeth clack together, and I'm shivering too much to shake out my sodden nightie. I should peel it off too—god knows it does fuck all to cover my body, and now it's heavy and drenched, clinging to my chilled skin. But something stops me. I'm alone, in a foreign place. I'm wet, and freezing. I don't want to be naked, too.

Rubbing the goosebumps on my arms, I look around. What now? Where do I go? Maybe I can find a little hollow in a bush where I can curl up and hide. Or some moss or something to dry or cover myself with.

The night has gone silent. Where there were sounds before—birds, insects, the pounding of hooves—now, there's nothing but the shushing sound of the waterfall. My heart thuds at a gallop. Too much running. I gulp in the cool air and press a hand to my chest. *Need to stay calm.*

A powerful sensation punches me in the gut. Warm tingles cascade over my chilly skin. There's a sudden, hot gush between my thighs a second before my clit starts to throb.

What the actual fuck?

My senses heighten as if the drug I took has kicked into overdrive: my vision sharpens to the point where I can make out the dark flowers on the vines growing up the trunks of trees. My nose prickles, taking in the aromas of the forest: a fresh scent from the running water, a loamy musk from the moss and earth, a piney, herbal scent rising from the river bank plants I crushed underfoot. Something smells delicious, like smoky, maple syrup-flavored bacon. My mouth cramps and I lick my lips, tasting the flavor in the air.

My nipples were already hard but now they're so taut, they're painful.

A coil of lust unfurls in my lower belly—so profound, it takes my breath away—and there's another hot gush from my sex as my clit thumps in sync with my pounding pulse.

I let out a moan, unsure whether it's one of terror, or desire.

There's a flash of movement in my peripheral vision and then I hear something that makes my blood run cold:

A low, nerve-prickling, gut-clenching growl.

It goes straight to my clit, making more fluid trickle down the insides of my thighs, and I let out another whimper.

What's happening to me? What the fuck is this?

An enormous shadow emerges from the foliage to my right. I'm frozen to the spot. The creature is huge—tall enough to blot out the moons, with rigid biceps bigger than my head—and it's the one who's growling. It's also the

17

source of that incredibly sexy smell... oud wood, and bonfires, and maple syrup smoky bacon...

My legs start to move without me even thinking about it. I run, blindly, my arms raised to defend my face from the branches as they whip at me. The wind chills my wet gown.

The roaring is growing louder, the scent stronger.

Still, I run. My core cramps and more wetness sluices down my thighs with each step.

This is nuts. And it's futile. The creature I saw was enormous, and his stride would make it ridiculously easy to outpace me. But I'm not gonna roll over and let him capture me. Sian may have wanted to be caught, but I sure don't. If this is one of those Alpha things she was talking about, I'd rather not find out what exactly he'll do to me when he catches me. And so I continue to sprint, forcing my aching legs to keep pumping.

I don't stand a chance.

Huge, thick arms grab me from behind, tugging me backwards. I slam against the enormous beast who caught me with no effort whatsoever.

He pulls my back to his chest, holding me in a grip of iron, still growling.

His rumbling makes my sex clench and throb. It takes a minute for me to register that he's actually speaking, saying the same word over and over again.

"Omega."

I'm whimpering. Sian said something about how the Alphas used to hunt the Omegas. Is that what's happening? Is this huge beast clutching me an Alpha... who thinks I'm an Omega?

"No!" I cry, twisting fruitlessly in his grip. "I'm not an Omega! Let go!"

"Omega," he rumbles again, and the resulting clench in my pussy takes my breath away.

I'm torn between abject terror, and animalistic lust. I can feel the beast's cock against my buttock, and it simultaneously horrifies and fascinates me. From what I can tell, it's just as huge as the rest of him.

Hot breath wafts over the juncture of my shoulder and neck. The Alpha is licking me. His tongue feels huge—broad, but soft—and I try to twist away, but then one of his hands comes up to grip my throat, and I freeze. To my relief, I can still breathe. He's not squeezing my neck hard. And yet just having his massive hand there does all kinds of things to me. It's weirdly reassuring and oddly paralyzing. I hang there, limp in his embrace, while he continues to lick the side and back of my neck... and then he nips it gently. I shiver, and there's another sharp pang between my legs.

Fuck my body for reacting this way. There's a deep, continuous rumble, like thunder. He's still growling. His massive chest is vibrating with the force of it. I'd love to get a good look at him but it's hard, what with him being behind me, and my lust-addled inability to concentrate. Still, the sound is reverberating through every fiber of my being, making me squirm—and want to clench my thighs around the tingling between them.

His scent is just as potent as the noises he makes. It's like a tangible thing, setting my senses ablaze. I close my eyes as his grip on me tightens, and then I feel like I'm falling.

He's pushing me down, moving with me to the forest floor. His hold on my neck has shifted, sliding around to my nape, and it's with a slow steadiness—and an unyielding dominance—that he forces me, first to my hands and knees, and then guides my torso even further down with a gentle push in the small of my back.

I follow his direction fluidly, as if hypnotized. Nothing exists but him, and the way he's making my body feel. Am I drugged out? I don't have the energy—or the will—to resist. The Alpha's rich, tangy musk makes me want to lick him back.

As soon as my cheek is pressed against the cool grass, my thighs are tugged further apart and then—holy mother of god—that tongue of his finds my clit, lapping at it with broad, wet, gentle strokes. He lifts my hips up a little higher to get better access, arching my back at an almost ridiculous angle, but I'm so lost in the sensation of his tongue on my pussy that I don't squirm away. I grip the grass to keep still. I don't want to fight. I want more.

Over and over, he licks that taut, throbbing little bead that has become the center of my entire world. Somehow, he's still growling, adding a toe-curling vibration to his ministrations.

I'm too aroused to breathe, digging my fingers into the dirt. I try to move my hips but he's lifted my lower half clean off the ground.

Holy shit, he's strong.

I'm so wet that, despite his growling, I can also actually hear his tongue swiping through my crease and over my clit, over and over again, and as humiliating as that is, it's also intensely erotic.

I'm just about to explode when he dips down and licks my entrance instead, tongue-fucking my pussy with short, delicious stabs, and I writhe, angling my hips this way and that, trying to get off but not quite able to.

A tiny part of me is acutely aware of what I must look like: face down in the forest floor, wearing nothing but a drenched, transparent negligee, my bare lower half hoisted rudely into the air and thighs splayed obscenely while I'm licked into delirium... but it feels so good, I don't give a fuck.

"Please," I mumble, but it's muffled by my forearm.

That crazy hot tongue of his is still slithering in and out of my pussy, and I'll die if he doesn't go back to my clit soon.

"Please..."

After several more moments of torture, my silent prayers are answered, and his tongue finds that pulsating little nubbin again. He licks me harder this time, and I'm exploding by the third stroke—a crescendo of pleasure radiating out from my sex and making me see stars. My pussy is clenching hard and fast, and I feel little gushes every time it squeezes the air.

I hear sobbing. It's coming from me.

The guy's tongue keeps me riding the peak for longer than I ever thought possible, but eventually the waves begin to abate and I let out a long, shuddering breath.

My clit is aching, rigid, hyper-sensitive...

...and he's still licking me.

"Ow! No!" I try to twist away, but my pushing and kicking are futile—he's so strong, if he decides I'm not going anywhere, I'm not going anywhere. "Fuck!" I'm swimming in mid-air, scissoring my legs in a pathetic attempt to escape his iron grip, but he simply holds me in place and keeps licking me ruthlessly.

It's the most delicious ache.

I stop fighting, allowing the sensation of his soft, wet tongue laving my clit to wash over me. Within moments, I'm close once more.

Can I come again so soon? Am I multi-orgasmic? I guess I'm about to find out.

Or not. When he stops licking me and flips me over onto my back, I scream with frustration. "Please..." It's a mere whimper. My voice is hoarse. My clit is pounding and I'm so desperate for release, nothing else matters. I just want his tongue on me again.

But for several long moments, there's nothing. No movement. Just that relentless growl, and the cool night air whispering over my drenched sex.

I've had my eyes tightly closed this entire time—at first, because he was behind me and I couldn't see him anyway, and then because I was so lost in pleasure. Now, I'm afraid to open them. Afraid of what I'll see. I know he's still here because that rumbling growl is still twisting my insides, somehow making more juice seep from my aching, empty pussy. I can feel it trickling down over my butthole.

I didn't know it was possible to get this wet.

"Mine."

At first, I'm not sure I heard correctly. How can he talk and growl at the same time? My eyes fly open. *Please don't tell me there are now two of them.*

The moons are behind him, his face is in shadow. But the silhouette of his enormous bulk is imposing enough. Thick, finely defined muscles stand out in stark relief against the lilac glow. It looks like the sides of his head are shaved, but a thick braid is falling over one broad shoulder.

He also has a dark, neat beard.

His eyes are hidden. I wish I could see them.

"Huh?" I manage, hoping he'll say more. "What did you say?"

"Mine," he says again. It's more of a grunt.

"What's yours?" I blink up at him, trying to concentrate despite the aching pull in my clit.

In response, his huge hands circle my ankles and he tugs me towards him, spreading my legs further apart and pushing them up and back.

I feel humiliatingly exposed and yet somehow, I want this. I know exactly what he's about to do and, god help me, I want it.

I want him.

FOUR

The Hunter King

THE PERFUME HOVERS in a cloud over my prey, a mouthwatering mix of juicy sweetness and musk. The moons overhead make her pale gold skin glow against the dark grass. My head spins like I'm in a dream, but this is real. This is a genuine Omega. Ulf knows how or why she's here, in my forest, in Arboron, but no matter.

She tastes right.

When her sweet, sweet slick hit my tongue, I thought I would explode right there, in my breeches. More potent than the strongest wine, her essence is dynamite to my senses.

My cock is harder than it's ever been. So big. So painful.

And yet she is such a tiny thing, so fragile, I must fight the urge to do as my body commands. Control myself.

An impossible feat for an Alpha in rut. And I am in rut. I am alone with an Omega who is in heat.

All things I never imagined possible. And yet... here we are.

Ulf has blessed me with a big cock, and I do not wish to

injure the Omega, so I wanted to pleasure her first. Make her wet. Acting on instinct, desperate to taste her, I did what I have done to countless Beta females, hoping she would enjoy it as much as they seem to.

She did. When I first licked that sweet crease between her thighs, she was already wet enough—but I didn't want to stop. I could pleasure her forever.

Her throaty cries and pleas were almost my undoing. And when she began to wriggle in my grasp, I had to force myself to keep licking her stiff little button long enough to renew her arousal after her climax.

A satisfied female does not crave cock.

I want this pale little Omega to crave mine.

Then she will *be* mine.

Now, she is on her back before me, her robe rucked up to display her lower half splayed open, wet and ready. I ache to be inside her. To fill her as completely as no male has done before. And yet, I must be cautious. I don't want to hurt her. As much as I wanted to throw her down and mount her like a beast the moment I caught her, she is too precious.

I'm grateful I released my cock from my breeches earlier, while the Omega was gushing over my tongue since both my hands are busy now, holding her slender little ankles up by her ears, opening her up entirely to my gaze.

I drink in the sight of her, wanting to etch it into my memory. When she opens her eyes and looks up at me, the desire on her beautiful face is unmistakable. She is an Omega, and I would have rutted her regardless, but the fact she so obviously wants it makes what I'm about to do all the sweeter.

Checking to make sure I'm still growling, I rock my pelvis into position, lining myself up with her little hole. I must go slowly.

It will take every ounce of control I have.

Once the head of my cock is kissed by her wet heat, I push inside—just a little.

Just the tip.

The Omega cries out, and I feel her sex fluttering around my rigid member.

Surely she's not climaxing again?

The thought makes me want to fall upon her and rut her with abandon, but I breathe deeply instead, pushing a little further inside.

Despite the river of slick cascading from her cunt, she's so tight, I can feel the stretch around me.

"Please," she whispers, but I have no idea what she's asking for. To stop? To keep going? To move faster?

I don't think she herself knows.

Ulf, but she feels good. My balls are heavy, tingling and, looking down, I can see the knot already beginning to take shape at the base of my cock. Her plump nether lips are parted, glistening in the moonlight. My cock looks huge between them. Will I fit?

Readjusting my grip on her ankles, I push a little deeper still.

The Omega lets out a low, guttural moan, and her cunt contracts, squeezing me once.

Hard.

My cock jerks at the sudden sensation, and she squeals.

I cannot wait any longer. Letting go of her ankles, I lean forward, placing my hands on either side of her head. Bending down, I lick the seam of her full, juicy lips until she parts them and I can kiss her properly. My tongue plunders her sweet mouth and, at the same time, I thrust my hips until I'm buried inside her to the hilt.

I drink down her screams as her hopelessly tight little hole is forced wide to accommodate my considerable girth.

Nothing in my life has ever felt this good.

I pause, savoring this moment of absolute perfection—her taste, her scent, her cunt squeezing me like a wet, skintight glove. I want this to last forever...

...and I'm desperate for release.

A lykka bird takes startled flight from a nearby bush. The sudden movement makes me rear up. I need to pay attention. I've caught a real, genuine Omega. It's the Hunt of the Moons. This forest is crawling with Alphas, several of whom will be looking for me by now.

And when they scent her? Even the worst hunter will be able to track us by her strong perfume.

My canines ache. I must mark her as mine, then hide her away—so I can rut her again and again.

Leaning back down and once again sealing my lips over the Omega's, I begin to move, pumping my hips in deep, measured strokes. Her cunt is out of this world.

I know I will not last long.

Sliding one of my hands between us, I grip one of her plump, round breasts, finding and rolling the nipple between my fingertips. The Omega groans into our kiss, and I feel her gush on me.

That tips me over the edge. Thrusting harder, faster, I give myself over to the sensations this little creature is evoking in me—all of them combining to the greatest pleasure imaginable.

It begins as a tingle at the base of my spine, then shoots through my cock like a thunderbolt. Her little pussy grows impossibly tighter. I've knotted her. She lets out a cry which reverberates through me, and then I'm roaring as I climax, pounding her into the dirt, jet after jet of my seed spurting from my pulsating dick, filling her to overflowing.

I never knew it was possible to come so hard. I almost black out.

After what feels like an eternity—and yet not nearly long enough—when I've emptied myself into her completely, I allow myself a moment to slump over her and catch my breath.

I'm spent.

I bury my face in the crook of her neck as I pant, my cock still tingling, my knot still sealing us together as one.

As we were designed to be.

There's a sudden crashing in the undergrowth nearby. We're in the forest, in the middle of the hunt. There are Alphas everywhere, pretending to search for an Omega yet never expecting to find one. They have scented the impossible and are coming to investigate. They are drawn to her, as I was.

If we stay here, she's in danger.

I snap my head down, sinking my teeth into the silky flesh where her neck meets her shoulder.

The Omega lets out a raw, ragged scream, and bucks beneath me. My cock jerks inside her, her inner walls clench rhythmically, and it hits me that she's coming, gushes of hot slick soaking my dick and seeping past the knot.

I lick the wound, tasting her blood, growling with a sudden, fierce possessiveness.

Mine. This Omega belongs to me.

I just claimed her.

The knowledge that a simple bite from me was enough to make her orgasm is so hot, I want nothing more than to stay here and rut her until we both pass out, but voices are echoing nearby. They're coming closer.

My subjects.

Alphas.

I must bring this female to safety. Luckily, my hidden lair is nearby.

I rear up and tug myself free of her soaked, swollen

cunt. A gush of milky fluid leaks from her as soon as I move, but there's no time to admire it, or play with it.

We must go.

But when I rise, I realize it's too late to escape. A cluster of Alphas have emerged from the trees. They're on foot, and standing mere feet away. The hunger in their eyes is mirrored in mine. The one closest to me—Golzon—lets out a low warning growl. His nostrils flare.

They can scent her. My Omega.

Mine.

I return the growl and tug up my breeches. The Omega curls into a ball, tucking her head down while the cloud of her dark hair covers her face. Her white shift is a moon-bright beacon in the night.

Golzon prowls forward, surrounded by his five closest friends. They fight like a pack, in a typical pattern I've seen many times. They think they are stronger when fighting in a group. It is their strength and their weakness.

Golzon and his pack look tough in the pieces of armor they wear to enhance their Alpha bulks. But underneath, they are soft as forest scuttlers, a bottom-feeding bug that makes an easy meal when I pry off the carapace to get at the meat.

True to form, Golzon breaks forward, facing me, expecting me to concentrate on him while his cronies fan out around me. A predictable move. They think there is safety in numbers. It will be a pleasure to show them how mistaken they are.

In the palace, they've never dared to attack me directly, but they've often murmured to each other how I am unfit to be king. Now is my chance to show them why I am the greatest Alpha in all the kingdom.

I must use caution. So much is at stake and I have someone to protect: the shivering Omega at my feet.

"What is it you have there?" Golzon asks. His voice is thick and feral, more growl than the proper speech he prides himself on. The Omega perfume hangs heavy in the air. These Alphas are close to being consumed by the rut. The Alpha madness will make their fighting styles more wild and unpredictable. It's more dangerous, but easier to get them to make mistakes.

Golzon growls when I don't answer, and draws his weapon. "You think you're too good for us. A worthy king," he sneers.

I don't bother to reply. Golzon will not listen. I cannot tell him why I am a superior Alpha. I will have to show him.

The Alphas who hang around the palace are entitled fools who have never known a moon-cycle of starvation. Never had to challenge the ulfine packs for a chance to hunt in the deepest wilderness. I did all these things when I was still a boy.

I would have taught Golzon the truth of what I am long before now, but the Betas at court would whine and fuss if I killed my own subjects. Brokk would counsel me to punish or maim the Alphas but not kill them.

Ulfdamn the rules. Golzon and his cronies are trying to take what is mine, and for that, they will die. I should take their eyes just for looking at her.

Golzon starts to circle me. I curl up my lip, flashing a canine.

"The feral orphan," Golzon sneers. "The barbarian. You're more animal than Alpha. Every time you open your mouth and grunt, we laugh at the Wild One pretending he can be king."

The Wild One. This is how Golzon mocks me. He thinks I am ashamed of being a savage. It is not my shame, it is my strength. These Alphas visit the forest but I am part of it, a living, breathing extension of its power. I am one with the grasses, with the creatures that fly or slither or creep through the thickets. One with the yaknos ferns, and the reaching vines of the cex trees.

An Alpha like Golzon can never understand. When he and his cronies go out to hunt, they find the biggest, proudest prey animal in the forest, then they stand back and let their arrows do the work. They don't get their hands dirty. And it is time to show them how a real Ulfarri Alpha raised in the wild can fight.

Golzon lunges forward, holding his weapon in an uncalloused hand. At my back, two of his cronies advance. The Omega at my feet whimpers. I must make this fast.

I allow Golzon's attack, turning so his blade slices a small chunk off my shoulder. Alphas like Golzon fear pain. They fight to avoid it.

I fight to win.

Golzon overbalances as if he didn't expect his blade to connect. I smash a fist down on his arm, and he loses his sword.

I whirl and rip my claws through the Alpha on my left. Blood sprays. The Omega yelps as fluid spatters her. The enemy with the torn throat falls, convulsing on the grass as his life ebbs away.

The other Alphas halt, clutching their weapons. They act shocked at my brutality. They have forgotten that Ulfarri are the Brutal Ones. I will not hesitate to sacrifice every one of these Alphas, my so-called subjects. If they threaten what is mine, they do not deserve to live.

"You killed him," Golzon says.

My growl reverberates around the grove.

"She's an Omega," another Alpha chokes out. "It's true."

Golzon attacks again. He's lost his weapon, but his claws are out.

I duck, dropping to all fours like the animal he says I

am. I race forward and cut him off at the legs. I flip him over my body, taking care to toss him as far away from the Omega as possible. He crashes into a tree and it shudders.

Two of the Alphas have slunk away, leaving Golzon and another two. The other two circle us, growling. Their musk pollutes the air. They want to rush towards the Omega, the source of that maddening, sweet scent. One of them is a hulking monster who's smarter than he looks. Too smart to be associating with Golzon.

The three of them dash at me, attacking together. The Omega has scrambled away behind a rock, leaving me free to rain down total destruction on anyone left.

I face the three, claws out and fangs bared. I leap onto the larger one and sink my teeth into his shoulder, ripping off his armor along with a chunk of his flesh. Blood fills my mouth.

The big Alpha roars as I leap away. I've slashed the straps of his armor. It offered little protection, but now he will feel exposed.

Golzon and the second are still attacking. The second has a blade. He rushes forward. I pretend I am as slow as an elderly Beta and let the blade almost touch my midriff. I grab his wrist and force the attacker to complete his lunge. His blade drives straight into Golzon's chest. I jerk it across. Golzon falls, holding his own guts. I kick the second Alpha's knee out of its socket and twist the weapon out of his hand to drive it into his throat.

There's one giant Alpha left. He's clutching his neck where my teeth tore a chunk out of him. He got off easy. His two friends are now corpses on the ground. He bows to me, backing away.

Smart warrior.

There's a sharp cry from the Omega's hiding place. Her pale limbs thrash in the hold of a dark shadow—another

Alpha. The coward was lurking on the outskirts of the fight and couldn't resist the opportunity to take what he wanted.

The Omega arches her body back, making it difficult for the Alpha to keep hold of her. She has no fighting skills, but she's trying. She slams her feet down to stomp on his foot. Her heel kicks up, catching the Alpha between his legs. The shock makes him stagger. It's enough for me to race across the clearing, dig my claws into his neck, and rip his head clean off. The severed head bounces over the blood-soaked grass.

The decapitated body falls. The Omega twists free. Her foot splashes into a dark puddle, and she chokes on a whimper.

I snatch her up. I want to race to carry her far from here, but instead I turn to show her the state of our enemies. Their deaths will soothe her.

"Y-you..." My little one's eyes are wide open, unseeing. "You k-killed them." Her teeth clack together.

Enough. I cradle my sweet bundle close and head towards the whispering stream I can scent in the distance. I duck around hanging vines and step lightly through the ferns. The grasses part as I pass.

The forest is calm. Far off, I sense the hunt ending. The Alphas have paired off with their Beta prey. Their pleasured cries have died away. They will have retreated to the palace for more revels, leaving the forest at peace. The creatures are returning to their work and play under the moons. The insects and night birds swoop, and sing their eerie songs.

The small leaves on the vines of the cex trees whisper this news to me as I find the stream and follow it until it widens to a river.

My Omega is still shivering when I set her down on the bank and wipe the offal of our enemies from her skin. I scrub my beard and slosh water into my mouth until the bloody taste is gone. I wade into the cool deep with her in my arms, and when we emerge on the other side, we are washed clean.

I head off, holding my Omega tight against me.

She's limp, silent, not resisting or fighting me in any way.

There's a strange tug in my chest.

Ignoring it, I press on, stalking along the river bank until the hushed roar of crashing water drowns out the creak and chirp of the night insects.

The silvery sheen of the waterfall glimmers ahead. My lair lies behind it, in a huge cave hewn by the elements.

Nobody knows it exists. It's where I come to hide from my duties. From society. Not even Brokk has found it, because I am careful to wash off my scent before I approach it. The thick herbs that grow on the river bank will cover the Omega's scent. We will be undisturbed here.

My chest is rumbling. I am purring to soothe her as I carry my precious bundle through the hidden entrance into my hideaway. The Omega is so still, so docile. Is she all right?

She is beautiful, with her pointed chin, the slight tilt to her nose, her lips swollen from my kisses. Her breathtaking eyes are closed.

Is she asleep? Unconscious? The kernel of worry gnaws at me. I lay her down on my fur-covered bed and she still doesn't move. Her limbs are cold and her hair hangs in wet strands. Our dip in the water washed away her perfume, but it's already returned, subtly scenting her skin.

I tuck the furs around her, lifting the sodden strands of hair away from her neck and fanning them out on the pelts to dry. I'm still purring for my Omega.

An Alpha's purr can soothe, comfort, even subdue his

mate. It's then that I realize: my little Omega—my lysia flower—is not hurt or insensible. She's calmed to my purr.

Instant relief floods me, and I waste no time in settling myself down beside her, wrapping her tight in my arms, pulling her against my chest.

She fits perfectly against me.

Now that I'm able to admire her in peace, I gaze my fill at her curves, her smooth skin, her dark, taut nipples pressing against the gauzy material of her tunic. She smells delicious—a combination of her own unique scent, and my seed. I lick my lips; my cock is rigid again already.

Soon, I will rut her the way she deserves to be rutted. I will bring her to climax until she passes out from the pleasure. I will fill her every hole, and cover her with my cum.

But first, I am content to lie here for a moment and let her rest, marveling over how much can happen in such a short while.

What a miracle this night has proven to be.

I am no longer alone. I have a mate. A queen. An Omega.

FIVE

Haley

THERE'S a searing pain in my neck, and I feel drunk. My eyelids are so heavy, it's an effort to lift them enough so that I can see.

I blink a few times, trying to bring my surroundings into focus. What happened? Where am I?

A shadow falls over me. I blink up at the giant holding me. The brute. The beast. The monster who chased me down and caught me, and who made me orgasm harder than I thought possible. The one who fought off the others who wanted to get at me. He's got a thick arm wrapped possessively around my midsection, and he's staring right at me.

When my gaze meets his, there's a searing twist of heat in my lower belly, and my traitorous clit gives a breath-stealing, prolonged thump. Who is this guy? And why the fuck does he have this insane effect on me?

I force myself to look at him—really look at him. He's rugged and rough-looking, with a broad, slightly crooked nose, a square jaw, and a generous mouth framed by a beard. Heat floods my cheeks at the unbidden memory of all the delicious things he did with that mouth, and I swallow hard, forcing the thought away. He has thick brows, one of which is bisected by a scar, and as I suspected before, the sides of his head are shaved. His remaining hair is long, and the braid which lies over one enormous shoulder is tied with some kind of twine. A bone-white, needle-thin fang as long as my middle finger hangs from a cord around his neck. Bronze markings swirl over his skin. Under the coppery tattoos, the rippling sheen of his muscles looks green.

Wait—what? I blink again. His skin has a greenish tint, the shade of wet grass. It has to be a trick of the light.

We're in a cave of some kind, with fourteen foot-high, rough-hewn rock walls and a rounded roof. Furs cover almost every available surface. A brazier sits in one corner, unlit. There's the steady sound of whooshing water... like a waterfall. Are we behind the waterfall?

There's more light in here than out under the moons, coming from glowing orbs which are dotted around the space—and they're freaking *floating*, suspended in mid-air.

Everything I've seen and heard ever since I woke up and encountered Sian is starting to point to a possible explanation for what's happened to me, but my brain can't even begin to countenance the idea. Aliens aren't real. I'm not on another planet. There's just no way. This must all just be a vivid dream. Or a Ren Faire run by overly enthusiastic organizers.

I return my focus to the hunter lying beside me. The one whose taste and touch do insane things to my insides.

His eyes suck the breath out of my body. Intense, hooded, fringed with long, dark lashes, they're a vibrant hazel. His stare goes straight through me, like he can see right into my soul.

It makes me uncomfortable.

It makes me wet.

"Where am I?"

He gives a grunt in response.

"Huh?"

Another grunt. His hand slides up my side, then around to cup my breast. My nipple responds immediately, growing tauter with every caress of his calloused thumb. The resulting ache between my thighs reminds me how soaked I am. I can't possibly want him again already.

Can I?

"Please talk to me. You can talk, can't you?" I'm sure I remember him saying at least a couple of words. "I'm Haley. What's your name?"

"Hey-leah."

Christ, when he says my name in that raspy, growly voice, my breath catches. "Yes," I say, encouraged. "And you are?"

"Omega. Mine."

"No!" Not another method actor! "You! Who are *you*?"

He utters another noncommittal grunt before twisting the nipple he was still playing with. The sharp slice of agony makes me cry out and, weirdly, my clit gives another languorous thump. The fuck is wrong with me? I'm getting off on everything this guy does to me? Literally *everything*?

I open my mouth to give him a piece of my mind but then his tongue slides between my lips and that woodsy, inherently delicious taste of him zings through my core. I find myself kissing him back with wild abandon, losing myself in his touch, his scent, in him. My hands wander over his enormous, ridiculously muscular body, exploring his broad shoulders, pecs, abs, rippling back—before sliding up to caress his head, pulling him to me to kiss me harder.

He responds with a toe-curling growl. One of his massive hands slides into my hair and grips it tight, while the other delves to that throbbing place between my thighs. His fingers are so thick, I can't tell how many he slides expertly up inside me, but when he finds a sensitive spot on the inner wall of my pussy and starts to stroke it, I can't suppress my scream of delight.

Each thrust of his fingers is making me gush anew, and I'm lying in a puddle—I can feel it coating my buttocks. When he slides his soaked fingers up to my clit and begins to rub it wetly, I go rigid in his arms. The first tingles of an approaching orgasm have already started, and I feel like it will be so intense, I'm almost frightened of experiencing it.

I'm vaguely aware that he's growling again. My arms prickle with goosebumps, but I'm not cold. Nothing exists but this hunter, and what he's doing to me. As he kisses me, his tongue is mirroring his fingertips, sweeping up and down, from left to right, circling with expert precision, every stroke stoking the flames of need in me until I'm trembling with it.

I'm on the edge. So, so close.

"Please," I beg, but the word is muffled by his mouth on mine.

His hand in my hair tightens, tugging harder right at the base of my skull, and the sudden sting tips me over.

I come, screaming, my entire sex rippling with the force of my orgasm.

I'm still coming when he lets go of my hair and darts down my body, sealing his hot mouth over my clit.

"Holy fuck!" I'm threshing and wailing, gripping the furs beneath me, and my screams go up a notch when he resumes finger-fucking me even as he's licking and sucking my pounding bud.

He forces me through so many orgasms, I lose count, with one blending into the next, blending into the next, until I'm incoherent, and too shattered to move.

Something warm and wet splashes on my face, and I open my eyes. The hunter's big hand is hovering over my face. The liquid is dripping from his fingertips, over my lips and chin. This is my juice—the result of all the orgasms he wrung from me. It's so depraved, yet so hot, and I open my mouth, tasting myself and something else: him. He came in me before, I remember. This is the sum of us.

I accept it greedily, surrendering to the pleasure.

When the broad tip of his impossibly huge dick spears my slick, aching sex, I groan for more. He's lifted my legs again but my thighs are together, my knees bent and pressed up towards my face.

With a deep rumble that goes straight through me, he forces himself all the way, deep up inside me. This position raises my hips and ass, but with my legs together, my pussy is even tighter than before, and holy fuck, do I feel every inch of him stretching me...

I want more. I writhe beneath him, pinned by his brute strength, helpless in the face of my body's reaction to him.

He fucks me slowly at first, pressing my closed thighs to my chest with his thickly muscled forearm, giving me no choice but to accept his cock.

I can feel my pussy trying to clench but I'm stretched so taut around him, I can't even do that—the mere thought of which is enough to push me to the edge again.

He increases the pace of his thrusts, going faster and faster until I see stars, and then he reaches down and drags his thumb over my hopelessly exposed, swollen clit.

I come with a scream—there are noises coming from me that don't sound human. They're raw. Primal. Desperate. They echo off the walls, providing a perfect foil for the rhythmic, wet pumping of that massive cock in and out of me, and the reverberating growl that makes the hunter's great chest rumble incessantly.

There's a searing pain in my sex and it feels like his cock's gotten even thicker, even though that can't be possible. This happened the last time he fucked me, too, I remember dimly.

And although the ache is sharp enough to take my breath away, I'm gushing again—or trying to. I'm so full, my pussy can barely even contract.

The hunter feels it too. He lets out a roar which makes the hairs on the back of my neck stand on end, and yanks his cock out of me with a rough tug.

I squeal at the pain, and the sudden feeling of emptiness. More hot splashes land on my bare skin—he's coming, thick ropes of cum spattering my face, my breasts, my pussy. Fuck, there's a lot of it... spurt after spurt... and for some reason, I'm so turned on by it.

I want to taste it so I do, bringing some up to my lips, licking it, closing my eyes. This is the hottest, filthiest dream I've ever had.

He's still holding me in that position; I can picture the round target my ass and pussy present for him, and now he's smearing his cum over my clit with rapid, precise strokes—the same cum I'm tasting right now—and it feels so good that, even though I didn't think it possible, he forces me to orgasm again.

The waves of pleasure crashing over me are so intense, everything goes dark...

SIX

Haley

WHEN I OPEN my eyes again, the hunter is beside me, holding me tight. I feel warm. Weirdly safe. Like I belong here.

Which is nuts.

He must have wrapped me in a fur while I was out cold. Did I fall asleep? God, he made me come so hard that I passed out. I didn't even know that was a thing.

Then again, nothing has made sense, not since I woke up practically naked in a forest.

I do a quick mental scan of my body. My pussy is throbbing, but it doesn't hurt. It's almost pleasant, but the desperate desire to come has abated. Thank fuck. The side of my neck is another story. It aches sharply, and I reach up to finger it.

"No." The hunter catches my hand, drawing it away. "No," he says again.

"You bit me!" I remember it all in a flash—the searing hot agony, and how the intensity of it made me come all over his cock, which was still inside me. "You fucking *bit* me!"

"Mine."

"Stop saying that!" I wish I had a mirror so I could see the wound. So I could see myself, as a matter of fact. I bet I look a mess—then again, who wouldn't after the night I've had so far? Not to mention, I'm covered in his cum... and quite a bit of my own. "I'm not yours. I don't belong to anyone!" *As far as you know,* a little voice whispers in the back of my mind. After all, I can barely remember anything about my life before waking up in the woods.

Seeing five moons...

A ridiculously tall woman with elf ears...

Being hunted like a damn fox...

Being fucked on the forest floor by a guy I just met a few minutes ago, before he stood up and *killed a group of warriors.* Killed them super dead. One guy lost his head.

I could chalk almost everything up to an elaborate Game of Thrones re-enactment, but actual beheading? That's taking the method acting too far.

I can't deal with it right now, so I stick the whole fighting part of the night into a file folder in my brain marked: *To be dealt with later.*

"Please talk to me," I try again. "What's your name?"

Turning to look at the hunter, I will him to meet my eyes. To my astonishment, he does. Then he looks away again and gives a noncommittal grunt. Goddamnit.

"If you don't tell me, I'll give you a name myself," I warn.

Silence.

"Fine. Have it your own way, Grunty McGreenface." I don't know where the hell that nickname came from, but it seems to suit him.

Immediately, he meets my eyes again and narrows his

gaze, his brows slamming down and a crease appearing between them.

"Don't like it? Give me your real name."

He gives a growl—a real, honest-to-god warning growl—and for the first time in his presence, I feel a genuine flash of fear. Then I check myself. *Honestly, Haley, what more can he do to you? If he wanted to kill and eat you, he'd have done that already.*

"Mr. Gruntypants," I continue. "I can come up with loads more."

"No," he says, and pushes me back down, rolling me onto my back without preamble, and pressing his lips against mine. The resulting pang in my pussy makes me gasp, but then my tummy gives a giant rumble. It's so loud, the hunter rears up and looks down at my belly, then back up at me, with an almost comical look on his face.

"I guess I'm hungry," I say sheepishly. I'm thirsty, too, come to think of it.

"Food," he says.

"Yes, please."

He rolls off the furs, and I'm once again astonished at how gracefully he can move, considering his size. Getting something out of a chest I didn't notice before, he brings it over to me before moving to the brazier and lighting it.

I glance down to see I'm holding a fruit like the one Sian gave me to drink from. Like I watched her do, I punch a hole in the top with my thumb and sip from it gratefully, letting the cool, sweet juice soothe my dry mouth and throat. I suck the thing dry, then wait until Mr. Grunty looks over at me. "More?" I say, holding out the empty husk.

He simply points to the chest and resumes what he was doing.

Pulling the fur he wrapped me in tighter around myself, I get to my feet. My bladder is cramping. I need to pee.

Fuck.

"Um," I begin, not sure how to explain this. "Do you have a restroom here?" It's a dumb question. There's no bathroom here. No door is visible. I don't even know where the exit is.

Mr. Grunty is holding something over the now blazing fire. Something on sticks. Some kind of meat. Skewers. My tummy rumbles again.

"I need to pee," I declare loudly, finally drawing his attention. "Use the restroom."

He stares at me for a long moment, then points to a corner.

"I am not going to do my business there!" I tell him emphatically.

He shakes his head and gets up. "Follow."

When we've gotten closer to where he was pointing to, cool air wafts in my face. There's a way out, hidden behind a rock wall. "Oh." I let him lead me out, then look around, hoping to find a bush or something.

He stands up straight and folds his arms across his massive chest.

"Oh no. You're not gonna watch me pee. That is where I draw the line."

"Safe," he says.

Safe? As in: he won't look? Or he has to stay here to protect me? Hoping it's both, I look around again. We must be at the back of the cave—I can hear the thundering water-fall, but I can't see it. There's a large bush to my left, and I hurry towards it, my desperation overcoming my modesty. "Don't look!" I tell him as I squat behind the foliage.

He gives a grunt. I can't see him, so I have to just assume he can't see me, either. When I've done my busi-ness, I look around for something I can use as paper. The leaves on the bush are broad and flat. Fuck it. Praying I'm not about to give myself some terrible rash, I use that, then return to Gruntypants's side.

It's getting light. The temperature has increased, and in the pink-streaked sky, the last two of the five moons are sinking below the horizon.

We're in some kind of forest, but it's not like any I've seen before. Trees rise like skyscrapers. Their bark is red and their leaves are black. Groves of neon-orange ferns glow between each monolith. Copper-colored rushes rattle by the river. Before I can gawk some more, the hunter has grabbed me and dragged me back into the cave.

Gesturing to the pile of furs we slept on, he stares me down.

"You need to work on your communication skills," I grumble as I head over there. "You're not giving great woo."

Ignoring me again, he gets back to whatever he was doing at the brazier. The smell of smoky meat tickles my nostrils, and my tummy rumbles again. Deciding to make myself useful, I head over to the chest and get out more of the fruits they use as beverages around here.

Mr. Grunty glances over to check what I'm doing, then returns his attention to cooking. I can't figure him out. Then again, I can't figure anything out right now.

Setting a couple of the fruits down for him, I sit cross-legged on the furs, and wait. I have so many questions. Like: where the fuck am I? Who is this guy? How in the world did he get me to let him fuck me?

Okay, so the answer to that one is simple. Feeling the heat rise in my face at the memory, I close my eyes and force myself to ignore the unbidden pang in my sex.

The hunter distracts me by bringing over a large, flat stone holding the food. The aroma of barbecued meat overpowers even his distinctive, delicious scent, and it's all I can do to wait until he's seated before reaching for a skewer. Following his lead, I gnaw at it.

It's surprisingly good.

For such a big brute, he eats with the same dexterity he displays when he's fighting. And... doing other things. Popping the top of another fruit, I take a sip before picking up a second skewer. The meat tastes like tangy chicken, and I force myself not to put any more thought than that into its origins.

We eat in silence. I don't know when I last had food, but I manage three whole skewers before I'm full. Grunty McGreenface puts away seven, plus three of the fruits.

"Thanks," I tell him. He can understand me just fine. Just like Sian did. He just doesn't talk much. It's infuriating.

Looking up from the empty plate, he meets my eyes, and my tummy does a little flip at the raw lust in his hazel gaze. I feel like I know exactly what he's thinking.

"Oh no," I tell him. "I need to wash first. And so do you."

Getting up off the bed, he leans down and scoops me up.

"No!" I squeak. "What are you doing? I can walk!"

Ignoring me, he turns and starts striding. My face is squished against his chest so I can't see where we're going. All I can do is wait until, a few moments later, he shifts me again, setting me down on cool grass. We're back on the river bank.

The humid heat settles over me like a damp blanket. Glancing up, I see three suns.

Wait. *Three?*

Why not? There were five moons last night, after all... if things are going to be weird, they may as well go all out, right?

Shaking my head, pushing all those thoughts away, I

examine the sparkling lake. It's a stunning turquoise color, so much prettier and more inviting than the murky depths I contended with last night. I can't wait to get in. I'm covered in the hunter's cum—and my own.

As if he can sense me thinking about him, he takes my hand and pulls me down the shore toward the water's edge. It's cool but not too bad. His fingers on my palm feel searingly hot by comparison, and I give a little shiver.

Side by side, we walk into the lake, until the water has reached my waist. The hunter pulls me towards him and begins to splash me. "Hey!" I protest, laughing, though it doesn't feel bad.

He frowns, as if considering something for a moment, before pulling me to him and dunking me down until I'm in up to my neck. He glides his hands over my shoulders and digs his fingers into my hair to scrub my scalp. He's washing me.

It's kind of sweet.

His skin is a richer green by day, glistening like the surface of an emerald. I stare at him, enjoying the soothing sensation of being washed gently and the chance to ogle him freely. His hair looked black. It's not. It's the dark, rich green of pine trees at dusk. The markings swirling across his skin like tattoos are a pale bronze, mirroring the copper flecks in his hypnotic eyes.

Get a grip, I scold myself. *Remember where you are. Remember what he did to you.*

Oh, god, yes. What he did to me. The way he lapped at my clit like it was the most delicious thing he'd ever tasted. The rush of desire which shoots through my groin makes me gasp aloud, and his fingers tighten on my body. Did he feel it too?

No way. That's not even possible.

Looking up—god, he must be almost seven feet tall—I

meet his eyes and they're dark with the same hungry lust I feel. Pulling me towards him, he lifts me effortlessly, holds my thighs painfully wide apart, and lowers me directly onto his hugely erect cock.

Even though there was no foreplay and we're in water, my sex is somehow slick enough for him to enter me, and I cry out at the burning pleasure as he stretches me to the point where I'm not sure I can take it.

It hurts so good.

His hands slide round to cup my ass, and his mouth crushes mine as I wrap my legs around his waist, his musky, delicious maple syrup bacon flavor exploding in my senses.

He begins to rock his hips slowly, bouncing me on his cock, my rigid clit being dragged relentlessly over his groin.

"Fuck," I manage, but it's muffled against his lips. His fingers are digging into my buttocks and the pain somehow only enhances the pleasure. I'm so close but I need it faster. I need something to tip me over the edge. "Please," I whimper.

His sudden growl is all it takes. I come, screaming, my pussy snatching greedily at his still pistoning cock. My arms are wrapped around his neck and my fingers are tangled in his thick hair as he drinks down my moans.

If he's noticed I'm coming, he doesn't show it. He just keeps on fucking me, kissing me, right through my orgasm, and straight on toward the next.

I'm on fire, my every nerve ending is ablaze. My clit is thumping, my legs are shaking. Just as well he's holding me up. Nothing has ever felt so good as what he does to me, and I somehow can't get enough of it.

One of his massive paws slides slowly up my back and then cups my nape, pinning my head in place as his tongue strokes mine in the lushest way. He's still growling, a deep rumble that vibrates through me.

There's a sharp, searing pain between my legs as I'm stretched even wider around him. I squeal at the burn but he simply starts to fuck me faster, harder, driving me relentlessly to another peak.

He's so big and thick that he's hitting all the sweet spots inside me, and when he tears his mouth from mine, his growl turns into a roar, and his cock jerks hard, I come again. My orgasm is so intense, I see stars.

He's coming too, I can feel him pumping what feels like gallons of hot cum deep into my fluttering pussy, prolonging my climax with every spurt.

I do the only thing I can do: cling to him and whimper as he wrings every last ounce of pleasure from my shuddering body.

Then I'm falling. The hunter is simply bending his legs, dunking us both in the water before straightening up and striding up the riverbank.

I'm clinging to him. He's carrying me. We're fused together by his knot.

"We haven't finished washing," I say, "we need to go back in."

As usual, the hunter doesn't reply. He lowers himself to his knees and leans forward until I'm on my back on the forest floor with his great bulk covering me. His teeth brush my shoulder. His fingers find my nipple and tug it until I let out a moan, and a hot rush of desire shoots through my clit.

Looks like he's not done yet.

SEVEN

The Hunter King

RUTTING this exquisite little female is without a doubt my new favorite thing. Maybe my favorite thing ever. The way her eyes widen with a mixture of shock and desire when I push my cock inside her slick, tight little hole—I can't get enough of that look. The sounds she makes when I pleasure her, hurt her, kiss her... the taste of her sweet honey musk on my tongue...

I'm addicted.

I never intended to fuck her in the lake but her sudden pang of lust went straight through me and I couldn't help myself. Somehow, I can tell when she is aroused. I can sense it. Smell it. Taste it.

All my life, I've fought and scrapped for what I want. But now Haley is here, a gift from Ulf. Like a ripe fruit heavy on the bough, bending until it hangs in front of my face. Perfect and sweet, easily plucked.

All mine.

I cradle her as we lie on the thick carpet of pungent herbs by the riverbank, joined by my knot. I should be spent, sated, allowing her to rest against me and catch her breath—instead, I'm still burning for her.

I want more.

Her tits are plump, round, they fill my palms with a lush, ripe springiness. I nibble one of her nipples, rolling my tongue around it, feeling myself jerk inside her with every breathy moan she emits. My fingers are pinching the taut bud which crowns her other breast. When I pull and twist it, she cries out and gushes on my cock.

My little lysia flower seems to enjoy pain.

This gives me an idea.

My knot is now soft enough that I can withdraw from her, so I do. Then I lift her gently to her feet.

"What are you doing?" she says. Her voice is breathless. "We need to go back in and—"

I kiss her, cutting off her words and forcing her backwards until she's standing up against a nearby cex tree. Its vines are soft and supple, but inordinately strong.

Haley doesn't resist when I turn her to face the trunk, then take her hands and lift them above her head, placing them against the smooth bark of the cex. The vines slide across, circling her wrists, holding her fast.

I cannot recall how old I was when I learned I could call the vines to me, nor did I ever discover how I came to possess this power. In the palace, I even forget I have it. Only when I'm in the forest do I feel the force and energy of the land. I rarely use this power these days, but in this instance, it's proving useful.

"Wait!" she cries. "What are you doing? What's with these vines?"

"Shhh," I tell her. I'm concentrating, telling the tree what I want. I nudge her bare feet further apart with my foot, gratified when more vines encircle her ankles. She is now naked and splayed out, unable to escape, giving me the opportunity to learn her and explore her reactions to my heart's content.

"Hey!" she cries again. "What's happening?" There's fear and anger in her—I can sense it, so I slide my hand between her spread thighs.

I'm immediately rewarded with a gasp of pleasure and a gush of slick into my palm. Using it for lubrication, I grind the heel of my hand against her pussy, marveling at how the stiff pebble of her clit contrasts with her soft, swollen lips.

"Fuck," she whispers, and my cock—rigid again—jerks at the thought of what I'm about to do.

With slow, steady movements, I bring her to the brink of climax. Then I remove my hand from her slippery sex and slap her bare ass, hard. The sound echoes off the trees, and she lets out a garbled cry.

Rubbing the handprint which is appearing on her smooth skin, I watch and listen carefully. I sense trepidation in the Omega, and a little ache, but also pleasure. Desire. She wants more.

I slap her again.

Then again.

Brokk once mentioned how he enjoyed doing this to females, and I'm beginning to understand why. The sounds my little flower makes every time I spank her are not unlike the ones she makes when I'm pleasuring her. Her plump ass is turning a beautiful shade of pink, and I'm filled with a sense of pride and ownership at the sight of my marks on her.

Reaching around with my free hand, I cup her bare cunt once more, using my hold to push her hips back while I continue to spank her.

"Please... please..." She's whimpering, panting, dripping into my hand as she grinds herself against me, rolling her hips in the most delicious, sensual way as she humps my palm.

As beautiful as her movements are, she must learn that her pleasure is mine to give, not hers to take. I wait until she's at the pinnacle, then I remove my hand from between her legs and dole out a flurry of blistering slaps all over her ass and down the backs of her spread thighs.

She lets out a howl of pain and frustration, and I bite back a smile.

This stunning creature is mine. My mate. My Omega. Mine to pleasure, to reward, to possess. Mine to discipline and deny as I see fit.

As I am doing now.

"Fuck," she whispers, her hips still moving as if seeking my touch. "Please. God, please."

I find her clit again, tracing tiny circles over it with the pad of my middle finger.

The Omega is rigid for a few moments, then she once again begins to move her hips, trying to regain control.

It takes three attempts—three times, I must remove my hand just before she's about to climax, then spank her bare ass and thighs good and hard for as long as I deem necessary to drive my point home—before she learns not to move when I'm pleasuring her.

When she finally remains still, I reward her, of course, sliding the entire length of my slippery palm up and down, up and down over her pulsing clit, moving faster and faster, until she cries out and convulses, her cunt snatching against my open hand, her slick dripping all over the place.

I milk her slowly, wringing every last shudder from her, until my cock is leaking and my balls ache with need.

Moving to stand behind her, I take a moment to admire the sleek lines of her back, the way her dark hair tumbles over her shoulders, the two little dimples above her ass, which is now a hot, deep pink.

Silently commanding the tree to lengthen the vines around her ankles to give me more room, I grip her round hips and tug her butt towards me, pushing her torso down a little so I have better access.

In one smooth, deep thrust, I'm inside her slick pussy. My left hand is still covered with her juice and I lean forward and reach around, smearing it over her lips, her face, her tongue.

She's licking her own slick off my fingers. A savage bolt of lust takes my breath away. With a growl, I begin to fuck her, pulling almost all the way out before plunging back in, stifling her cries with my cum-covered hand.

Ulf, she feels so good I can hardly stand it.

Reaching around her with my other arm, I tug her hips back and towards me, lifting her feet clear off the ground. There's something about the way her legs dangle in the air on either side of me that drives me half mad. I felt the same way when I was licking her before.

Her ankles are still encircled by the vines, and so are her wrists—she's still bound to the tree. I tell it to tug her legs further apart so I can rut her even deeper.

She screams against my hand as the knot begins to form and I push it up inside her tight little hole. Her legs are almost obscenely splayed now, and the sight of her, bound and helpless, dangling by her wrists, held up only by the vines I command and my rigid cock as I thrust into her again and again, is almost my undoing.

Her little forbidden entrance winks at me as she undulates, and I vow to take her there too. Slipping a finger into her hot mouth, I growl louder as she sucks it. Once it's nice and wet, I bring it to her back hole, and push, popping in to the first knuckle.

I'll be damned, it's even tighter than her cunt. Her rear whorl is spasming—snapping uncontrollably—and so is her pussy.

She's coming.

Sliding my finger into her asshole obviously pushed my little Omega over the edge.

With a roar, I follow her, my finger screwing its way further up inside her as I climax. Showers of sparks flicker behind my closed eyelids, and hot pulses of pleasure make my cock jerk inside her, filling her with my seed, staking my claim. Her cunt is overflowing with it; it's spilling out past the knot, coating my groin and thighs, pooling on the forest floor.

Gripping her tight, my cock in her pussy and my finger in her ass, I ride my little lysia flower until we're both spent and panting, and every last orgasmic drop has been wrung from us.

I help place her feet back on the ground, then pull her up so her back is to my chest. I hold her tight, nuzzling her neck, breathing her in. Her scent makes my head reel.

I don't know what I did to get so lucky but now that I have this perfect little Omega, I will never let her go.

She is mine.

Forever.

EIGHT

Haley

HOLY FUCK.

I didn't know anything could feel this good. The hunter may not be a big talker but he gives the best orgasms.

When those vines crept around my wrists and ankles, binding me to the tree, making it impossible for me to escape, I had a moment of sheer panic, but then...

I'm dazed, and my limbs feel heavy. My butt is sore from his slaps but even that feels good somehow. Tingly. There's a river between my thighs.

I sag, limply, not resisting when he scoops me up and carries me back down to the river's edge. Cradling me to his enormous chest, he wades into the water and washes me gently. I cling to him like a child, breathing him in. Why does his deep rumbling purr make me feel so calm? It's similar to his growl but has a completely different effect on me. The growl makes liquid heat rush to my groin, whereas the purr...

It makes me want to purr, myself. My eyelids feel heavy, and there's a pulling sensation in my chest. Most of all, I need to touch him, to be near him. It's a compulsion I can't explain.

His fingertips are soft on my wet skin, and I marvel at the contrast between the savage way he spanked, edged and fucked me, and the way he's handling me now, swishing away all the cum—both his and mine—that's soaked my lower half.

A hot rush floods my cheeks as I think about what he did to me just now... the way he spanked me every time I tried to grind on him until I realized he didn't want me to move, and the way he slid a thick finger up inside my butt with no warning, no apology.

The second he did that, my orgasm came out of nowhere, blinding me, snatching the breath from my lungs so I couldn't even scream with the force of it.

I have questions—so many questions—but no energy to ask them.

I doubt he'd answer, anyway. I still don't even know his freaking name.

Once he deems us both clean, Mr. Grunty carries me back to his hidden cave behind the waterfall and lays me down on the furs. I whimper when he moves away, mad at myself for craving him so bad but unable to stop myself.

He stokes the fire, pulling out a handful of dark, weirdly shimmering reeds he must have collected when we were by the river. I don't know how he had time to do it while rocking my world, but I guess he did, and I didn't notice.

He twists and turns each reed over the fire, as if tempering it. I'm too tired to sit up but fold my hands under my head so I can keep watching. He's half turned towards the fire, half toward me, and the flickering light makes his markings writhe like snakes over his epic muscles. Or maybe I'm just half asleep.

He pokes a reed at his upper chest.

"Oh." I cringe away. He's threaded the reed under his green skin, somehow. He grunts, turning his head my way, but keeps threading the reed through until he's made some sort of design on his left pectoral muscle. When he sets the reed down, the shape of the design remains, the dark color shimmering on his skin.

He's tattooing himself. He continues until he's marked his left pec with all the reeds, and tossed the remains of his makeshift needles into the fire. He returns to my side and, tired as I am, I lift a hand to touch his chest. I'm careful not to press the area he just marked. He's tattooed a design of seven teardrop shapes in a circle. The ink shimmers darkly, like an oil slick. It looks a little like a flower.

"Lysia," he tells me. I nod because I don't have the energy for a conversation of grunts and one-word sentences. It'll take too long to figure out what he means.

He takes my hand and presses my palm to the tattoo. I cringe for him—the skin must be tender—but he presses his hand over mine.

"Lysia," he says again.

"Lysia," I repeat, and he seems pleased. He lies down and tugs me against him.

With dream-like slowness, I stroke his face, tracing the scar bisecting his eyebrow. He has humanoid features, other than that brilliant green skin. His musk is the yummiest scent I've ever smelled. If I weren't so tired, I'd rub myself against him. But I've already done enough of that.

I drop my hand and curl into his chest. He's still purring. With his huge arms wrapped around me, his warm breath on my hair, and his earthy, masculine scent surrounding me, I can no longer fight off my exhaustion. I close my eyes and slide into oblivion.

When I wake up, there's a moment of confusion. What the fuck is this? Why am I in a cave? I look around, and it all comes back to me in a rush.

Now I know for a fact I wasn't dreaming... but the only other explanation is still too terrifying to contemplate, so I push it out of my mind and concentrate on the present.

Grunty McGreenface is still clutching me to his broad chest, and when I crane my neck, his eyes are open. Has he been watching me this entire time? How long was I asleep for?

"Omega," he says.

I suppress a sigh. I mean, a man of few words is one thing... "Haley," I say. "And you are?"

"Mine."

"I doubt that's your name. Where are we? Why won't you talk to me? I know you can understand me!"

He lets out a growl and then his lips come crashing down to sear my mouth. I lose myself in the intensity of his kiss for a second before pushing him away.

"Look, the sex is amazing, but I think my pussy needs a break, okay?" *And I need to find out where the fuck I am, and what to do next.* After all, I can't spend the rest of my life in a cave being brought to screaming orgasms by the brooding green giant.

Even though that's exactly what my pussy wants.

His hazel gaze is hypnotic and I stare at his face, somehow unable to tear my eyes away. His pupils are huge. What with his size, his green skin and coppery tribal markings, the growling and purring, weird cave dwelling complete with floating glow-orbs, and the freaking knot in his massive dick, I can no longer deny the reality that there's no way in hell this guy is human.

But then... what is he?

"Where am I?" It seems like a safe question. Besides, Sian already told me, so I have a way of verifying whether he's being honest.

"Mine," he answers.

Goddammit.

"I met someone. She said we are in Arboron. The Forest Kingdom."

He grunts. I guess that means yes.

There's a sharp pain as my teeth find my lower lip. Maybe I should quit with the questions. Never ask a question you're not prepared to hear the answer to. Not sure where I heard that, but it seems like sound advice. "How did I get here?"

Silly Haley. How would he know? He just found you in the forest. While out hunting. For Omegas. Which he thinks you are. As I thought, he remains silent on that one. I sigh.

"So... Arboron is the forest? And it's a kingdom."

"My kingdom." His tone seems sad, somehow, and there's another tugging sensation deep in my chest.

"Your kingdom?"

He places a hand on his chest. "King."

"You're the king?"

He nods.

"No freaking way." It slips out and I blush. Is he offended?

"King," he says again.

I take stock of the cave once more. It's comfortable enough, I guess, for a room carved out of rock, but it's hardly a palace. No plumbing. No aircon. No fridge. I prefer glamping. "Hardly a palace."

"Not palace," he says. I'm stunned. This is the most in-depth conversation we've had so far, and I'm desperate for it to continue.

"You have a palace?"

He nods, his expression grim. I get the impression he's not a fan, but can't tell whether it's being king he doesn't like, or this palace we're talking about. Maybe both.

"Will you take me there?" I blurt. A palace implies luxury. Soap. Food. People. Maybe somebody more talkative, who can tell me what the hell is going on. Like Sian— if she ended the hunt okay. She said she wanted to get caught. Maybe I can ask someone about her at the palace. "Please?"

He seems to consider it for a moment, then his expression grows fierce. "No."

"Why?"

His only response is to tug me tighter to him, as if I'd tried to get away.

"Why?"

"Mine."

I frown. He sounds like a toddler with their favorite toy when he keeps saying that. Does he want to keep me all to himself? Before I can think any more, he slides off the furs and tugs me to my feet. "What are we doing now?" I ask.

As usual, his reply consists of only one word. "Food."

Haley

Oh god. Oh god, oh god, oh god. Mr. Gruntypants is about to kill an animal, and he's making me watch. I swallow hard, fighting the wave of nausea that threatens to make me heave.

A short while ago, he led me out of the cave and through the forest, once again impressing me with his ability to be so agile despite his size. We had just emerged from a thick

61

grove of ferns when he stopped short. I plowed into him. His green brows knotted together.

"You didn't have to bring me," I muttered, defiant.

He brought a finger to his lips, then pointed. A weird looking animal was standing in a clearing. It was nibbling the leaves off a branch, displaying a long, slender neck. Were it not for the fact that it had six legs, was bright blue, the size of a sheep, and covered in stripes, I would have likened it to a giraffe. The long, curling tongue was certainly the same.

Now I'm frozen to the spot, watching with dread as the hunter—how apt and serious that moniker seems now—produces a weapon. It's like a snowflake made of steel or some other kind of metal, with each spoke consisting of what looks like a lethal blade. Where the fuck was he hiding that? I'm wearing a tunic he gave me which I'm assuming is his, since he's bare chested.

I look away, and close my eyes for good measure. Sure, I eat meat, and for all I know, that roasted deliciousness on skewers earlier was made from that exact same kind of animal, but I'm too much of a wimp to actually watch my food die.

A sharp elbow to my ribs makes me gasp, and I open my eyes to glare at McGreeny. He gives me a pointed stare, then lifts the weapon. "Throw," he whispers. It's barely audible but I understand him perfectly.

I shake my head.

"Throw!" he orders me again, more forcefully but just as silently.

I fold my arms across my chest. I'd probably cut myself trying to hold it. Even if I wanted to, there's no way I could throw that bladed star with any kind of skill.

And I don't want to.

Holding out his massive palm, the hunter shows me

how his thumb and middle finger are curved over the glittering blades before pulling back his arm to throw.

I've had enough. I'm not staying to watch that animal die. So I do the only thing I can think of.

I run.

There's an explosion of sound behind me—a roar, which undoubtedly came from the hunter, and a high-pitched squeal, which I don't want to think about.

Crashing through the undergrowth with branches whipping at my face reminds me of that first night. Was it only yesterday? The day before? I've lost all sense of time. Maybe even that is different here.

Regardless, I'm done. I don't care how amazing the sex is, I need to get away from Mr. Grunts, and find someone who actually has answers for me. Someone more talkative. Hell, a parrot would be more talkative than the supposed king who is now probably hot on my tail.

Another pterodactyl-like screech, infinitely more terrifying, rises from a bush directly in front of me and I rear back, skidding to a halt.

A creature leaps out to face me. It's the size of a large goose, but black with neon yellow spots. Forget pterodactyl. It looks like one of those dinosaurs which can spit sticky poison. It bobs its head, pointed teeth bared, its whole body rigid and tense, about to attack.

I damn near pee myself. "Shoo!" I yell, looking around wildly for a weapon. A stick. Anything.

It gives another eldritch screech, and takes a bobbing step towards me.

I whimper. A shadow falls over me, followed by a delicious maple syrup scent. The hunter is behind me. "Help me," I whisper. "Please."

He lunges for the animal, and I look away, unwilling to watch even this thing be killed. An outraged squawk draws my attention, and I glance back at McGreeny to see he's picked the thing up and is cradling it with something akin to tenderness.

"What the fuck?"

The animal is giving contented little squeaks, and nuzzling its downy head against the hunter's massive palm. Then it fixes me with huge, adorable eyes.

"A baby?" I mutter, incredulous.

The hunter nods, then looks up and around before setting off.

I follow him, staying a few paces behind, adrenaline still coursing through me. When he signals me to stop, I do, waiting and watching as he creeps forward a few more feet before setting the baby creature gently down on a patch of grass.

He's so tender, it makes my chest hurt.

Then he retreats, walking backwards to where I'm standing, as sure-footed as if he had eyes in the back of his head.

A few moments later, an ear-splitting shriek rents the air, and I clutch the hunter's arm as a creature I can only assume is the baby's mother swoops down on huge, leathery wings. With long, curved talons, she snatches the infant off the ground and flies on, disappearing into the lilac sky.

Lilac? How did I not notice that before? I guess I was distracted by the multiple suns.

I let out a long, shuddering sigh. "Thank you," I tell the hunter. I don't know how much danger I was actually in—maybe the baby animal wasn't as toxic as it looked—but the way he rescued me and handled the situation was something else.

One thing's for sure, he has a good heart.

"Come," he tells me, and takes my hand.

I expected to be scolded for running away, for not

staying to watch him make his kill, but all he does is lead me back to the cave. We have to go past the clearing where we sighted the giraffe-like animal, and even though I had promised myself I wouldn't look, I can't help it.

A swift glance tells me all I need to know: he felled it. God knows how precise his aim has to be if he can bring down an animal that size with a weapon the size of his hand, but I refuse to think any more about it.

Once we're back in the cave, he gets more drink-fruit out of the chest and hands me one. "Food?" he asks, and I shake my head. My stomach is still roiling. I'm thirsty but not hungry.

"No thanks," I tell him.

I slurp the fruit dry, staring at the shadows flickering on the walls of the cave. This place is too cold and bare. I could pile the furs up in the corner and burrow beneath them. It would be warm, although something would be missing. But what?

I have a sudden longing for a bed of unicorn stuffies. Weird thing to want, but maybe I'm craving a reminder of home. Even though home is a far off memory, like a movie I watched long ago. A movie I liked but have no real attachment to.

The hunter is squatting in front of me. He's been there for some time, watching me like a wolf watches a rabbit. I'm so out of it, I didn't notice. His brow furrows and he touches my cheek. There's a surge in my lower belly. I want him. I could easily get wet for him. But the cave is too chilly and something's... just not right.

The hunter leans forward, concern in his hazel eyes. I look away.

He rises and moves swiftly around the cave, dousing the fire and extracting a fur from the pile of them.

"What are we doing now?" I ask in a listless voice, not expecting a reply.

He approaches me, and wraps me in the fur, pressing an unexpected kiss to my forehead. Then he throws on a long, green cloak with a deep hood so his face is in shadow when he finally answers me. "Palace."

"Really?" A palace sounds promising. Maybe there, I'll finally get some answers.

NINE

The Hunter King

TAKING the Omega's little hand, I lead her out the back, secret entrance to my cave lair, relieved to see my tyrlee has answered my call. As long as she is within a certain distance, I can call her with my mind, just as I can make the vines move. I speak to the forest and the forest speaks to me. I learned this language before any other.

Last night, lying with my Omega in my arms, I remembered a mother whispering to me, tucking my small body against her soft warmth. She sang to me.

I have not remembered anything like that in a long time. I've lived so long in the forest, it became my home, my mother and father. My connection to it fades when I return to the palace, but it will never be severed. No matter how many people call me the Wild One and think I'm a barbarian. No matter how the councilors whisper behind my back about my strange ways.

At the thought of them waiting for me back at the palace, I suppress a shudder. Going there is the last thing I want to do, but the cave is too primitive for my delicate lysia flower. She needs warmth and a place to nest.

Besides, I have been gone for too long now. I need to show my face to remind them that I'm still alive. Brokk will be wondering what happened to me.

"What is that? Will it bite me?" My Omega is staring at my tyrlee with a wary expression on her beautiful face. I suppress a grin.

"No." *I am the only one who will bite you. You are mine.*

In the short time since this delicate female entered my life, I have been overtaken by a protective instinct stronger than anything I've ever felt. I would do anything for her. I would die for her. After a lifetime of feeling disconnected from others, I finally feel like I've come home.

Is this what they call the soul bond?

Her melodic voice interrupts my thoughts. "Will it carry both of us?"

Taking her in my arms, my nostrils flaring at her scent, I lift her carefully, and seat her on the tyrlee before getting astride the mount myself.

The Omega gives a little squeak as I make a clicking noise to the animal and we set off. I wrap my arms around her, marveling at how right she feels within my embrace.

This is where she belongs. Right here. With me.

I push back the wave of dread at the thought that we're heading to the palace. There will be other Alphas. Will they be able to control themselves around my new mate? I've given her the claiming bite, but I don't know enough to know whether this will be enough to deter them. If any Alpha should touch her, they will die, but I do not want to have to kill anyone else.

Now I understand Khan's behavior at the Council of Kings when I scented his Omega. At the time, I thought he was overreacting. If I was skilled with words, I'd seek him out and ask him how he keeps his *majesta* safe when she has to be around other Alphas.

Or I could keep my Omega locked up, to keep her safe.

No. No creature should ever be confined, unable to breathe free air or feel the suns' light upon their skin.

"Is it far? Are we going to the palace?"

I'm deliberately maintaining a slow and steady pace on the tyrlee so as not to startle my lysia flower, and she seems to have settled enough to resume her chattering.

I've never known anyone to talk so much—at least, not to me. She has so many questions, and I have no answers.

Once again, I am the idiot orphan. Feral. Never belonging. I could open my mouth but my replies would be nothing but stuttered grunts. More animal than Ulfarri. Shameful.

"I could do with a bath. Does anything like soap exist in this place? Ugh, I have so many questions. What are you going to do with that animal you killed? You just left it there, in the clearing!"

There's a pang in my chest. She thinks I'm capable of killing for pleasure. Never. I kill to protect my people, and for food. No other reason is ever good enough. "Food," I tell her. I stumble over the words, but force them out in a grunt. "Meat for my men." I'll send my men to collect it. Usually, I would bring home the kill myself, but I saw how upset she was at the mere sight of the carcass, and wanted to spare her.

"Oh."

I wish I could see her face.

"Your men? So you really are king?"

"Yes." It feels like an interrogation, and I suppress the urge to growl. *She's merely curious*, I tell myself. Just because I'm not comfortable with words, doesn't mean she feels the same way.

Her plump ass is nestled against my groin, jostling with every step the tyrlee takes, and my cock has once again stiffened in my breeches. I must still be in rut, to be aroused by such a simple thing. Will I be able to concentrate on anything when it ends?

Right now, all I want to do is turn around, hasten back to my cave, lay the little female out on my furs, and—

"Oh my god, that's so pretty!"

I look to where she's pointing. It's a lykka bird, perching on a nearby branch. They are beautiful with their impressive teal, violet, blue, and gold plumage, and curved silver beaks. They're also vicious creatures, especially during mating season, known to bite unwary intruders.

I understand their instincts.

It's odd, how I can sense my Omega's emotions. Right now, she's feeling excitement, apprehension, and a tiny lick of lust.

She lets out a groan. I've let my hand wander to that sweet, slick spot between her legs. I wasn't even aware I was touching her there. The feel of her soft, wet folds reminds me what it's like to be buried deep between them, and I let out a growl of pleasure as my cock jerks.

My fingertip catches the stiff bead at her apex and she stiffens, then lets out a shuddering gasp and gushes into my hand. I've never known a female to be so responsive. My chest swells with pride at the knowledge that I can make her climax with the mere swipe of a single fingertip.

It's a heady kind of power.

I'm so hard, it's painful, and all I want to do is tug her off the mount, throw her to the ground, and rut her again, but alas, we have arrived at the palace. I slide my hand further up, to her belly, to resist the temptation to make her come again.

"Fuck," my Omega breathes, and I don't know whether

she's still coming down from her orgasm, or exclaiming over the wooden structure which towers above the treetops.

My mind is still on how her taut stomach feels beneath my palm, and how it would be to feel it rounded, swelling with my progeny. To breed her.

The tip of my cock is oozing at the thought. Ulf, I'm hard.

"Is that the palace?" Her voice—thankfully—pulls me from my thoughts again.

I give an affirming grunt. I take a deep breath, mentally preparing myself for the ordeal. I hate the palace. It's comfortable, of course, and as king, my every whim is indulged, but for one: they never leave me alone. It's a constant barrage of questions, requests, pleas... and it makes my head ache.

"It's... not what I expected."

I look more closely as it comes into view, trying to see it through fresh eyes. Her eyes.

Built from wood and stone, it is large and comfortable, but not as breathtaking as the Wanderer King's waterfall-riddled structures, or as garish as the Golden King's gaudy monstrosity. The wood from the tallest trees has been hewn and polished to make the frame. The rest is grey and black stone. When I became king, vines appeared overnight, crawling out of the forest to cover the outer walls. The courtiers complained, and the servants tried to cut them back, but they simply regrew.

The clanging of a bell announces my arrival to anyone within hearing distance, and for the umpteenth time, I curse the councilors for not allowing me to cancel that stupid tradition.

"Majesty!" A Beta rushes up and takes the tyrlee's reins. His pale eyes run briefly over my Omega before darting back to me.

Suppressing a sigh, I dismount, then help my little lysia flower off the animal. I hadn't even thought about how to introduce her.

First things first: see to her comfort. Then I can find the councilors and let them scold me.

Brushing a stray lock of dark hair from my Omega's exquisite face, I press a kiss to her forehead, then ask her, "Bath?"

My mate's resulting squeal of excitement is music to my ears. In that moment, I know I would do anything to make her happy.

Anything... except let her go.

TEN

Haley

MY EYES ARE on stalks as Mr. Gruntypants leads me through the huge rooms of his palace. It's a weird combination of wood and stone—kind of natural-looking, but with jarring little things that remind me that this is a strange place. Glowing orbs, suspended screens, and paintings which move contrast sharply with the long, hooded robes the people are wearing, and the way nature seems to have taken up residence in the palace, right down to vines growing within the walls.

To my relief, the hunter whisks me past the robed people coming up to ask him questions—grunting is his only response, *quelle surprise*—and leads me straight to what looks like a solid wall of rock. He marches up to it and pauses, and it magically rolls open to reveal a long, low-ceilinged room. To the right is a massive four-poster bed, covered in cushions and furs. The knot in the center of my chest loosens.

Once inside, the hunter backs me up against the wall

and claims my lips. He pins my hands on either side of me. His deep growl triggers an earthquake of arousal in my core.

How can I want him again? Still? Always? Why does he have this insane effect on me? Why is my reaction to him such that a mere touch of his fingertip can make me come, no matter how weird the circumstances?

I'm panting, staring up at him. My core pulses but more pressing than my lust is my burning curiosity. Everything in me longs to explore the room and the bed. Especially the bed. And I want the bath that was promised me.

But I have questions, and I want answers.

"Sian," I say carefully, once I've screwed up the courage. "I want to talk to Sian."

He raises a thick, pine-green eyebrow.

"I met her that night... the night you found me. I want to see her. Do you know her? Can you find her?" During the ride to the palace, I spent a lot of time thinking about my next move, and Sian's face kept appearing in my mind's eye. Since the hunter is the king, and Sian wasn't far from the palace when I ran into her, I figured it was worth a shot. If he doesn't know her, maybe he can find her somehow?

His eyes are hazel pools of mystery. I can't read him right now. At all. It's infuriating.

"Please," I continue. "I want to learn what I can about this place. About Arboron." *About you*, I add silently, biting my lip, willing him to say that he either knows who Sian is, knows how to find her, or knows someone else I can talk to.

This seems to be working, I can see it in his eyes. "Sian?" he says.

"Yes! Do you know her?"

He gives a grunt and seems to think about it for a moment before he says, "Wait," and disappears.

I make my way to the huge bed—a California king is a dog pillow compared to a Forest King-sized mattress. Everything in this room, this palace, is huge. Perfect for the hunter. Way too big for little ole, human me.

Sinking down on the bed, I let out a little huff. How is Mr. Grunty so attractive and so infuriating at the same time? Has he gone to find Sian now? In an ideal world, he'd answer my questions, but he has trouble with speech. That's okay, there are other ways to communicate. We were starting to figure out how to commune in the forest, but since we've arrived at the palace, I can feel him pulling away once more. The question is, why?

It's a puzzle I'm determined to solve.

He returns a few minutes later with a familiar figure gliding along behind him. I squeal like I'm seven. I can't help it. "Sian!"

"Haley." The hunter used my name one single time and never again, and I'm startled at how moved I am that Sian remembered it. How nice it is to hear it. My eyes well with tears and I blink them back. "Are you all right?" she asks. She's standing a few feet away now, regarding me cautiously, her eyes constantly darting back to the hunter. He makes her nervous.

"Please leave us to talk," I say to him, hoping I sound polite but firm. I don't know if I can have this conversation with him standing there, staring at us.

For what feels like an eternity, he stands motionless, and I have a sinking feeling that he's going to say no. Then a look passes between him and Sian, and he turns around and goes.

I blow out a breath. Sian's shoulders relax.

"How did he find you so fast?" I ask the most burning question first.

"I work here, at the palace," she says, flicking her long, gleaming hair over her shoulder. Now that I can see her clearly, in the bright glow of the floating orbs, I can confirm that she is indeed green—albeit a different shade to Mr. Gruntypants—and her ears are as pointed as I remember.

"Did you... did they catch you? At the hunt?"

A tiny smile flickers around her mouth. "Yes. They always catch me. In the end."

"Were you hurt?"

"Only a little. It's what I signed up for. Betas who participate in the Hunt of the Moons know exactly what will happen when they're caught. I enjoy some pain with my pleasure. And I like the thrill of the chase."

I clear my dry throat. "He caught me. The... king?"

She gives a knowing nod.

"What's his name?"

"I don't know," she tells me. "We just call him *Your Majesty*. He is known as the Hunter King."

"You don't know his name?"

"No one knows who he is or where he came from. One day, during an intense Slythin attack, he appeared."

"What?" I sit down heavily in a nearby chair, stunned at this revelation. Then I remember my manners. "Please." I gesture to the other chair.

Sian perches herself in the seat with an innate, elegant grace. "Should I start at the beginning?"

"Oh god, yes, please." It's hard to hide the sudden wave of emotion as it threatens to overwhelm me. "I have so many questions. The king... doesn't talk much."

She rearranges the folds of her pale yellow gown. "No, he doesn't. There was a time when we didn't think he talked at all. Several years ago, assassins killed the last Forest King. We don't know which kingdom they came from—"

"Wait, there are other kingdoms?"

If she's frustrated, Sian is kind enough to hide it. "We are in the kingdom of Arboron," she begins again, "on the planet Ulfaria. There are several kingdoms on this planet;

Arboron is just one of them. Each kingdom is ruled by a king—the Wanderer King, the Golden King, the Hunter King, the Beast King, the Stone King, the King of Ruins, the Shadow King, the Demon King, the King of the Wastes..."

"Is that all?" I blurt. Then, realizing that may have sounded snarky, I add, "How many kingdoms are there?"

"There are nine official kingdoms, but there are also great swathes of Ulfaria which have yet to be discovered. The magicians tell us it is a big place."

"Seems like it." An ornate silver jug sits on a table beside me, with two matching goblets. "Drink?"

Sian shakes her head, so I pour just one, for myself. The liquid is tart and slightly bitter, but not unpleasant. It soothes my parched mouth.

"Okay, so there are several kingdoms. This is the forest kingdom," I say.

"Yes. So the previous Forest King was killed by enemy spies, and his Omega queen disappeared. The kingdom was in turmoil."

"Who killed the king?"

"No one knows for sure. But we think it was the Stone King, acting covertly to take our kingdom for his own. The Stone Kingdom lies on our borders. The king who rules there, the Stone King, is wily and a powerful mage. He doesn't attack directly. He uses magic and poison, assassins and spies."

"I see."

"Once the king and queen were gone, the kingdom was in chaos, overrun by Slythin."

"Slythin?"

"They're huge, terrifying creatures which slither on their bellies and have long, sharp fangs."

"Like snakes?"

"Snakes?"

I suppress a sigh. "Never mind. So, the Slythin are attacking. Then what happened?"

"The Hunter King just appeared out of nowhere. He was young, wild, barely a man grown. He was some kind of orphan, an outcast who never spoke, and lived in the woods." She leans forward and whispers, "They called him the Wild One." She straightens back up. "He took a sword, vanished into the forest, and conquered the Slythin single-handedly, reclaiming the forest and our kingdom. Came back bearing the biggest Slythin-tooth anyone had ever seen. It's mounted in the Great Hall. The people were so grateful to be saved, they crowned him their new king."

"Wow." My mind is reeling, trying to absorb all this new information. "What happened to the kidnapped Omega queen?" I'd love to talk to another Omega since that's apparently what they think I am.

Sian gives a little shrug. "She was wounded when her mate the king was killed and disappeared, never to be seen again."

"And no one investigated?"

"The Stone King has great magical powers," Sian says with a shudder. "There was no way to question him without offending him and risking war. We couldn't risk it. The country was already weak from the Slythin attacks. At least, until the current king came and banished them somehow."

"How did he banish them?"

"No one knows. He went into the forest and returned with a great fang. Proof of his triumph."

I can totally imagine the hunter doing that. Warmth swells in my chest. I place a hand over my heart.

Sian presses her lips together, suppressing a smile. "Our king is the greatest warrior in the kingdom. A good hunter, as well."

"Yes, he is." I murmur. "Is it hot in here?" I grab my cup

and gulp down more of the sweet liquid. "But he doesn't talk much, does he?"

"He can talk. He just doesn't, much," Sian says. At my disappointed look, she adds, "He will if it's important to him."

Great. I guess I'm not important enough.

"No one knows his name?" I ask.

"It's possible he doesn't even remember it," Sian says. "No one knows who he is or where he came from. There's no record of his family. He is truly the Wild One."

The Wild One. Yeah, that tracks.

"And he is the greatest warrior of our time. No one has seen a Slythin for years—until now," she goes on.

"What?"

"The king is not yet aware of this, but there have been sightings recently. A lot of people are worried. Arboron is a comparatively small kingdom. Mostly forest, not many villages. Word spreads fast. We export medicines and food to the other kingdoms, too, so we're often among the first to hear news." She sits back and regards me coolly. "Now I have some questions for you."

"Huh?"

Her ears twitch. "How did you come to be in the forest that night? It's clear you're not an Ulfarri. Who are you? Who sent you? Did you come to seduce our king?"

"Huh?" I say again. I'm in shock. Her tone has changed swiftly, from gentle to accusatory. "Nobody sent me. I was hoping you'd be able to answer my questions! I don't know how I got here, and I can assure you, I haven't set out to seduce anyone. If anything, it was the hun—the *king* who seduced *me*!" My cheeks flare hot, and I'm not sure whether it's due to outrage, or the sudden unbidden memory of how the hunter licked me that first night.

"Hmm," Sian says, looking wholly unconvinced.

"You're an Omega. You didn't just materialize out of thin air. Someone must have sent you."

"If they did, I have no idea who, or how, or why!" I say. "I woke up in the forest, and you found me. I don't remember what happened before that!"

"You remember nothing?" She doesn't seem skeptical, just curious.

I run a hand over my head. My hair is full of leaves and twigs, and now it's standing up on end. "Bits and pieces. Like, brand names and things. But a lot of things are hazy."

"I wonder if this has something to do with the other Omegas," Sian says thoughtfully, tapping her pointed chin.

"Other Omegas?" I bleat. What the hell is an Omega, anyway? It feels too late to ask.

"Omegas are the natural, perfect counterparts—mates —for Alphas," Sian says. "While Alphas can mate with Betas—like me—they cannot get them pregnant. Nor do they go into rut. Only an Omega going into estrus can induce the rut—and the ensuing knot—in an Alpha. Unfortunately, there are barely any Omegas left on Ulfaria. There are rumors that there are still a few in hiding, but I've never met one, nor has anyone else I know."

"Estrus?"

"The heat cycle. They get immensely, uncontrollably aroused—"

"Oh. Yes." I interrupt her before she can go into any more detail on that. "But I'm not an Omega! I'm a human!" Even as I say it, I can barely believe these words are leaving my lips. That I'm stating my species. That I'm even having this conversation.

"The Wanderer King found a Hoo-man Omega on his travels, and brought her back here, to Ulfaria," Sian tells me. "The Golden King, upon finding out that it was possible, commanded his magicians to recreate the technology, and bring him a Hoo-man Omega, too. And they did."

I blink, trying to wrap my head around this massive information dump. "Are you telling me there are two humans here? On Ulfaria?"

"Yes." She cocks her head, regarding me, her huge, beautiful eyes solemn. "At least... three, now."

If I'm not mistaken, it has just been confirmed that I am, indeed, on an alien planet, and that, for whatever reason, the people here believe I'm an Omega. That's the bad news —well, some of it. The good news is that I'm not alone. There are two others here who are just like me.

I'll be damned.

"Where are they?" I manage.

"With their mates. In the kingdoms of Altrim and Aurum."

"Are they far?"

She gives a little laugh. "Yes. They are both far."

Damn.

"I don't know how you came to be in the forest of Arboron on the night of the Hunt of the Moons, but it is a sign," Sian continues. "An omen. You are meant to be with the king. And I see he has already claimed you."

"He... what?"

She points to the spot where my neck meets my shoulder. "He bit you there?"

"He did." I close my eyes, remembering how hard that made me come. The wound healed fast, but it still twinges sharply now and then.

"That is how Alphas claim their Omegas for life. How they forge the soul bond. Can you sense him?" She cocks her head again, regarding me curiously.

I think for a moment. "Now that you mention it, I do sometimes feel like I can tell what he's feeling."

She nods. "That is the bond. You are his mate now. His queen. Now he's found you, and you are his Omega. It's so romantic."

Ugh. "Okay, so this Omega thing. What am I supposed to do?" I ask.

Sian's ears twitch again. "Do? You don't have any duties, per se. You attend to the king like we do. But there's no job or specific duty for you, other than to bear your mate's children."

"Kids?" I squeak. I put a hand over my belly. I've been filled with enough hunter jizz to fill a bathtub. At this rate, I could be pregnant with sextuplets.

Why does this thought fill me with contentment? I should be making an exit through the nearest wall. *Tiny grunty babies.*

"Yes. You will bear the king's children. They will be Alphas or Omegas. It is so romantic."

There's a twist in my lower belly. The thought of babies is making me horny. Goddammit.

"It's less romantic when you're sore," I mumble.

"Oh!" Sian claps her hands. "There are salves for that! I looked in the archives and there are all manner of balms and unguents to help Omegas to stay in full health. I recreated the rituals for my own pampering—I can show you. Come." She waves me to follow her through a set of curtains on the far side of the room.

My gasp bounces off the stone walls. Sian has led me to a bathing chamber.

ELEVEN

The Hunter King

ULF ONLY KNOWS why my little lysia flower wanted to talk to Sian, but the Beta was easy enough to find. I had thought it would be much harder, but all I had to do was say her name, and she was brought to me. Turns out she works in the palace.

I don't recall ever seeing her before, but then I tend to tune most things out whenever I'm here at the palace, with all the people chattering at me.

Now, I'm standing outside the door to my own chamber, listening to the conversation Sian is having with my new mate.

When I was a child, I would venture out of the forest, drawn by the scent of meat and grain roasting over a fire. To the villagers, I was a wild-haired, muddy creature who loped forward on all fours. An animal. They threw stones at me until I ran away. But the winters were cold and bitter, and I could not survive without the heat of a fire. I learned to live on the edges of the gatherings, lurking with the shadows, stealing what warmth I could.

And now I lurk outside my own kingly chambers, secretly soaking in all I can from my Omega mate. Her light, her warmth.

I must do everything I can to keep her. I will not survive without her fire.

I listen closely. I want to know exactly what's going on in my Omega's head, and she might speak more freely without me there. I want her to be happy, as her smile lights up my insides like a thousand suns.

I bristle when Sian talks about my childhood. My mate is upset because she thinks I refuse to speak. I must try harder. I cannot summon words as easily as Alphas like Brokk, or my Beta courtiers. It's not that I don't want to talk to her. I just communicate better with my scent, my lips, and my eyes.

My little flower is bursting with questions, and I feel a pang of guilt for not telling her more, myself. I don't know why I struggle so. But I've never felt this way for anyone before...

Then the Beta mentions recent sightings of the Slythin, and I ball my hands into fists. I never could prove the connection between the Stone King and the Slythin, but that twisted fuck was responsible. He must have sent them again—but why now? After all this time? So many moons have passed since I last defeated them, sending them slithering back to the Stone Kingdom.

I finger the fang I wear on a cord around my neck as a constant reminder.

Could it have something to do with my Omega appearing out of nowhere?

Or is it all merely a coincidence?

When Sian turns the tables and accuses my Omega of trying to seduce me, I'm torn between outrage and laughter. But the Beta does have a point. Where did the Hoo-man come from? Until Sian mentioned the other two Omega queens, I had forgotten the name of their species.

Hoo-man.

Haley.

My little lysia flower.

I must protect her—and the Arborii people—from harm. From that miserable creature, the Stone King.

Why would he be sending so few Slythin to skulk about the forest? It seems more like a scouting excursion than an attack. What are they looking for?

My instinct has never let me down before, and even as it tells me the answer, a sickening quiver twists in my belly.

They're looking for the Hoo-man.

My mate.

Suppressing a roar, I spin on my heel. Right then, the person I was going to find comes ambling down the passageway, reeking of the refreshment hall and Beta pussy.

"There you are!" Brokk says, taking a deep slug of sour-smelling wine from a curved horn. "We thought you'd been lost in the forest forever."

I hold up a hand to silence him.

Brokk blinks. His expression immediately changes from one of joviality to one of earnest intent. He drains the horn and tucks it into his belt. "Where do you go when you vanish for days at a time? Did you find a hot little Beta female to hunt down after all?"

"No," I tell him. I hold a finger to my lips and point to the closed door. Brokk starts as he hears voices.

"Who's in there?"

I shake my head and set off for the expansive gardens, assuming he will follow me. He does.

When I first met Brokk, he stuck to me like a burr sticks to my breeches. He dogged my steps, but it took several hunts for him to prove himself to me. Now he is my second-in-command. But can I trust him?

"Slythin?" I ask as soon as we're far enough away from everyone so as not to be overheard.

Brokk sighs. "Yes."

I wait for him to explain. I lean against a tree, folding my arms. A vine curls close to me.

"Half a dozen within the last few sun-cycles," he says. "Give or take. I've been waiting for you to return from the forest so I could tell you about it. The people are getting worried."

I reach out to brush the soft petals of a stunning kiya blossom.

"Who is in your quarters?" he tries again.

"Queen."

Brokk's head jerks back. "What?"

I grit my teeth but can't stop my grin. "Omega."

"Omega." Brokk breathes the word like I've imparted a rare and precious secret. Which I have. If words came easily, I'd share with him the story of how I came across this mythical creature during the Hunt of the Moons, and claimed her. But I only grunt. "Mate. Mine."

Brokk's mouth flaps open. He shuts it, then it hangs open again. The eloquent Alpha, so smooth at speaking to any lady, is speechless. He tugs on his turquoise beard, which he always wears in a single long braid, adorned with little silver beads. "I can't believe this."

I shrug.

"Am I to believe you found an Omega on the Hunt? And claimed her?"

I nod, pleased. Brokk could always read me better than anyone.

"That's wonderful news!" he chokes out. "You have a mate. An Omega, no less." He claps his hands together, looking more like a Beta courtier than a burly Alpha warrior. "We must plan the celebration. We must formally introduce her to the people as soon as possible."

I growl before I can stop myself. I don't want anyone to look upon my Omega but me.

Brokk's used to my grunts and growls. "The Arborii people deserve to meet their queen. But I understand, you wish to keep her safe."

Yes.

"It is a dangerous time," Brokk says. "There are more Slythin sightings now than the first time, before you took the throne. And our last queen, an Omega, was stolen when her mate the king was killed..."

My canines sharpen as if I've sensed a threat. No one will touch my Omega and live.

"We have no proof, of course, but if that is the case, you should introduce your new queen to the Arborii as soon as possible." At my questioning grunt, he adds, "You cannot hide her away forever, nor would you want to."

I give him a look. To hide Haley away forever is exactly what I want.

"All right." Brokk tosses up a hand. "Your Omega will not want to be kept in hiding forever."

True. My little lysia flower enjoyed my cave home, but she soon grew restless.

"Besides," Brokk continues. "The more Arborii people who know she exists and is here, the more there are to protect her."

He has a point. But not everyone is trustworthy. What if she is betrayed?

"I would like to meet her," he says. "I don't think I've ever seen an Omega before."

The possessive snarl leaves my lips before I can stop it.

"Peace, my king," Brokk says, raising his hands to show

me he is unarmed. "She is your mate. I would never touch her." He lowers his voice. "We found the bodies of Golzon and a few others in the forest. Your scent was there, along with another more puzzling one. The Omega leaves a strong perfume."

I bare my teeth. "Mine." I refuse to explain why I killed Alphas from my own kingdom.

"Right," Brokk says. "We figured there was a fight over a female. The court will understand." He sees my face and grimaces. "I know you don't give an ulfdamn about the court."

He's right. I don't. I hold his gaze until he drops his eyes.

"What's it like? The rut? Is it as uncontrollable as the legends say?" Black bleeds into his blue eyes, and his Alpha musk grows stronger. "I never thought I'd see the day where there was a real Omega in Arboron. Ulf has blessed you."

"Hmm." Ulf knows, I am lucky, but with that immense good fortune comes immense responsibility. My bond with my Omega is a weight in my chest—a sweet burden, but a burden all the same. She is so fragile. A Hoo-man. She could not survive alone on this savage planet.

My tooth slices my lip and I savor the biting taste of my own blood. She will never be alone, I vow.

"So... what *is* it like? The rut?" Brokk is babbling now, giving voice to all his curiosity even though he knows I won't answer. Can't answer. Wouldn't, even if I could. "Did you claim her?" At my nod, his eyes gleam. "Do you now feel the bond?"

I hum assent and press a hand to my chest, rubbing at the source of the constant tugging sensation. An invisible tether ties me to her, pinching when she is unhappy, flooding my heart with warmth when she is feeling contentment and joy.

"You have a bond." Brokk's black pupils have swallowed

up the blue in his eyes. He licks his canines as if they're throbbing to sink into the side of an Omega's throat. I know the feeling.

"I thought Omegas were a myth." He tugs his beard, looking lost. "Do you think there will be more now? Rumor has it that the Golden King is looking for a way to bring many Omegas to Ulfaria."

If I hadn't been present at the King's Council, to which the Wanderer King brought his new mate to show us, I wouldn't have believed Omegas to be real. But will there be enough for Brokk to claim a mate?

I shrug.

"The magicians sent word that King Aurus has been successful in his mission to bring more Omegas to our planet—at least, one more. His new queen." Brokk toys with the beads in his beard. "Do you think that's where your new mate comes from? Maybe she's one of Aurus's..."

I growl. "Mine." If the Golden King thinks he will take my Omega, I will rid him of the delusion. Aurus already has an Omega mate. Why would he want more? Then again, rumor has it he does have a harem...

"Or maybe she was meant for you. Why else would she appear at the hunt?"

I shrug again.

"No doubt we will uncover the truth in time." Brokk straightens, dropping his hand. "What are we going to do about the Slythin? You should address the people."

It's my turn to tug my beard and rub my face. What in Ulf's name are the advisors good for if they can't take on unpleasant tasks for me? Like this one? I growl even as I nod.

"I will set up a court appearance, my king." Brokk steps back and bows like a Beta courtier.

I force my shoulders down when they'd otherwise

hunch. If I had my way, Brokk would not call me king. I have no friends, but if I did, he would be one.

I brush past him, knocking him off balance so he steps out of his bow.

"Go on then," he calls. "I'm sure you want to get back to your Omega. Ulfdamn your luck."

I mock snarl at him but he's laughing. I spin around and lope towards the palace.

My little lysia flower is waiting. The ghost of her perfume fills my lungs. I cannot remain away from her for a moment longer. Her scent is all I can breathe, and my heart beats in echo to hers.

TWELVE

Haley

THE BATHING CHAMBER is filled with a floral-scented mist. I lie in a stone tub that could hold five people. The tub filled up once Sian turned on the seven faucets. The water gushing in was a weird green color but it smelled divine, and when I stuck my hand in, it was warm.

Sian left me to it, and I luxuriated in the water until the knots in my neck and shoulders melted away. She reappeared holding several bottles in different shades of blue and teal, which turned out to be different bath soaps, scrubs, lotions and salves.

I insist on washing myself, but Sian is sitting and chatting beside me while I relax under the bubbles.

"Here, try this." She dumps some pink liquid into my palm. It foams with a delicate, jasmine-like scent.

"This smells amazing," I say.

"Doesn't it? It's another recipe I found in the archives. Very popular with the former queen. It's too bad Omegas have all but died out."

"There are none I can talk to?"

"There are none left around here. There were a few a generation ago. But none have been born in my time."

"It's just so weird." I lean back against the edge of the tub. The smooth, rounded stones are perfect for lounging. "Did any of your doctors or, uh, healers and magicians look into it?"

"Of course." Sian folds a large cloth that looks like Turkish towel, propping it close so I can reach it without stepping from the bath. "It's all Alphas talk about sometimes. Alphas are obsessed with Omegas." She gives me a pointed look, and my cheeks grow hot.

"Yeah, I got that." I let bubbles sift through my fingers. "At least, they're obsessed with claiming one."

"Well, yes. But you should be proud. The Hunter King is like no other. He is a skilled warrior, but he prefers to be alone. He disappears into the forest for days at a time. Does the bare minimum to act as a king. But he's still a good leader," she says.

That doesn't mean he'll be a good mate.

Sian excuses herself, and I play with the bubbles with pruny fingers. After god knows how long in the forest, sleeping in a cave, peeing behind bushes, and washing in a river, soaking in a warm bath feels almost as good as sex.

Almost.

Nothing compares to sex with the Hunter King. My inner muscles are sore from taking his knot, but just thinking of him, a warmth blooms in my core.

I rub my shoulder with a cloth to distract myself, and a twinge makes me wince. The bite mark on my neck is still tender. I turn my head and there he is, strolling into the bathing chambers, parting the mists from the hot bath. He's in his usual attire of breeches and a bare chest. Water droplets lick down his bare pecs, adding a sheen to his green skin. The snake-like copper markings ripple on his skin, and the vivid flower tattoo stands out starkly, drawing my gaze like a magnet.

In a dreamlike state, I lift my hand and beckon.

His eyes hold mine as he shucks off his clothes. He steps into the bath, the broad head of his cock pointing right at my face.

I don't think. I scoot forward, and close my mouth around my Alpha's cock.

The Hunter King

My Omega is a vision: golden-skinned, and glowing in the bath. Her dark hair falls like a river down her back. She rises to her knees, angling her head as she puts her mouth on me. I dig my fingers into her hair, tugging her head back a little so I can see her face. Her eyes are closed, water beading on her black lashes. Her small hands rest on my thighs. As she sucks, she swirls her fingers along my markings, exploring their twisted paths up and down my legs.

My knot pulses and I tug her off, turning her and positioning her on her feet, bent over with her hands on the side of the tub. I kick her feet apart and slide my cock into her sweet folds.

As soon as I breach her entrance, her head flies back. Our mingled groans echo around the chamber. Her skin is covered in new, delicately scented unguents, but nothing compares with the mouth-watering perfume blooming in the air, driving me mad. She's so tight, I rock my hips, slowly gaining inch by perfect inch, until my thrusts threaten to lift her off her feet.

I hook one arm around her hips and cradle her chest with my right arm, holding her in the ideal position for me to thrust. She lets her head fall back, resting against my newest tattoo. Sometimes, on a new moon, I carve out more designs on my body, but I never marked the place over my heart. Not until I met Haley. My Omega. My little lysia flower.

She is my heart. She is my everything.

I cannot tell her, so I will show her.

I double over, draping her over the edge of the bath, still cradling her body against mine. My knot swells, hooking behind her pelvic bone, joining us together. Her hips twist, and she lifts her leg, somehow accepting more of me.

"Oh god," she whispers. "I've never been so full."

A balloon of warmth fills my chest. If I could just stay like this forever, hugging my Haley close, with my knot inside her, things would be perfect.

A drowsy smile quirks her lips. "I'm think I'm going to call you Hunter," she murmurs.

I lick my lips. I must not lose her. I must find a way to speak. But when I look at her face, no words escape. There's nothing for me to do but purr, and hope that she feels my love for her as deeply as I do.

Haley

A sharp rapping startles me awake. Beside me, Hunter rumbles, and his warm weight leaves the bed. I roll, wincing at the twinge between my thighs, and wrap myself in a blanket.

"My king," says a smooth voice. "I hate to disturb you but you are late—"

There's a grunt from Hunter. I sit up as he pushes whoever's disturbed us out the door, and shuts it.

"Who was that?" I ask without thinking. Hunter doesn't answer me, and I don't expect him to. He heads to a wooden wardrobe in the corner that's intricately carved with a forest scene. When he returns, he has a set look—determined, a little withdrawn. He was broody enough when we were alone in the forest. I had hoped we could connect now that I have more information about him, but right now, the tension between us is even worse. I rub my chest to ease the tightness.

Hunter hands me some folded material, and I look down at it.

"Dress," he says gruffly.

"Okay. Now?"

He just stares at me until I relent, and unfold the shimmering fabric. It's a floor-length gown in a rich teal color, with bronze accents on the hem and cuffs. It's sumptuous and almost regal. It will also completely cover my arms and legs. Naked, I scramble out of bed—he's seen every inch of me naked by now, so there's no reason to be shy—and slide the dress over my head. It fits perfectly. Did he have it made for me?

But how would that work without anyone taking any measurements, and besides, we've only been back a little while...

There's a flicker of something that looks like appreciation in his hazel gaze once I've got the gown on, and I feel a surge of pleasure. Is it something to do with this whole Alpha/Omega/rut/estrus thing, or the bond which is making me so desperate to please him? I don't do it consciously, but when he does register his approval of me somehow, I get a fluttering sensation deep in my belly.

"Come," he says, then turns, obviously expecting me to follow him. With one last look at the comfy bed full of cushions, I do.

He leads me down the hall from his bed chambers to an enormous room with a mounted, high-backed chair carved of astonishingly pretty wood. A throne. There's a smaller chair beside it on the dais, but it doesn't match its larger counterpart, and it was obviously placed there hastily. For me.

Once we're both seated, he gives a nod to a green-robed servant in the corner, who opens the giant double-doors.

A veritable sea of people rush in. The sudden noise is overwhelming. Hunter must sense my apprehension, since he takes my hand and grips it.

Trying to distract myself from the clamor, I look over the people's heads, admiring the artwork on the walls. I don't know how they make the paintings move, but the images are stunning—tumbling waterfalls, trees with rustling leaves, shimmering lakes...

In one corner, mounted on a huge stand, is what looks like a sculpture shaped like a tooth. I remember what Sian told me about the Slythin—how Hunter conquered them, returning with a giant fang. *That can't be it.* It's tricky to judge from this distance, but that tooth in the corner must be six feet long—possibly more.

I glance over at the huge man who's sitting beside me. His shoulders are hunched, his face impassive. I can feel his unease. He was an orphan, right? Sian said he grew up in the forest. He probably didn't learn to talk until he was older, and even now it seems to be hard for him.

He can talk, Sian said. *He will if it's important to him.*

A flash of longing for the forest, the cave, the wide open and wild spaces, shoots through me. I don't know if it's from Hunter or myself.

I wriggle on the throne, trying to get comfortable. But everyone is staring at me. I grip Hunter's hand, hard.

Once the room is crammed with people, a hush

descends, and another giant man gets up onto the dais to speak. He has a braided turquoise beard, and an authoritative manner.

"The king has returned," he proclaims, "and he has brought with him our new queen: an Omega."

Countless pairs of eyes swivel to scrutinize me, and I drop my gaze as if I'm super interested in the ground right in front of my feet. My face is getting hotter by the second. I'm so glad I was given this long gown to wear. I just wish it came with a mask, and a hood as well.

"All hail the Hunter King and his new queen!" Braided-beard shouts, and everyone repeats what he just said, in unison.

My ears are ringing.

Queen? Is it that easy? Just proclaim someone a queen, and they are? No marriage ceremony, no coronation...

... no fucking *consent*?

"I don't want to be a queen," I mutter, but my whisper is drowned out by the chorus of excited voices.

Braided-beard then turns to me. "You are most welcome here in Arboron, *majesta*," he says. "I am Brokk, second-in-command to your mate..."

My mate. *Mate*. I repeat the word in my mind, trying it on for size. Right now, I'm too overwhelmed to decide how I feel about the thought of having a *mate* whose name I don't even know. Who seems to only be interested in me for one thing—as amazing as that thing might be.

"We have called this audience so some of the people can air their grievances, and ask the king for advice," Brokk continues.

I slant another glance at the handsome but surly man beside me. Advice? From him? They'd have more chance getting golden eggs out of a goose.

"Would the first petitioner please step forward?" Brokk then steps off the dais, leaving us to it.

The Ulfarri are all exceptionally tall, way taller than humans. They also all seem to have brightly colored skin and strange, tribal, tattoo-like markings in different, contrasting shades. Having seen Sian and then the hunter, I had assumed they would all be green, but far from it. Although many of them are wearing hooded cloaks over their clothing, I spot a range of gorgeous colors—from pink to orange, blue to lilac, and everything in between.

"There have been more sightings of the Slythin," a woman begins, stepping up to the foot of the platform and removing her hood to reveal kingfisher blue hair and turquoise skin. "I'm afraid to let my children go out to play. What is being done about it?"

Everyone looks expectantly at Hunter, sitting beside me. So do I.

He looks like he would rather be anywhere else in the world. *Why be king if you hate it so much?*

I look over to Brokk for help, and he mercifully catches my eye, and comes to the rescue. "We are fairly certain it is not an attack," he says loudly. "We are looking into it, and will resolve the issue shortly."

What a vague, faintly reassuring response. He could be a politician back on Earth.

Still, what he said seems to be enough for the woman, who gives a little nod and takes a step back.

Another petitioner speaks up. "Where did the Omega come from? There has not been an Omega queen in Arboron in years!"

"Aye, I thought they were extinct," someone else calls out, and a chorus of murmurs breaks out.

Again, I look to my so-called mate to respond, but he so

obviously loathes being in the limelight like this, I feel a sudden burst of protectiveness.

"You thought so, but here I am!" I say gamely, to a smattering of laughter. "I certainly don't feel like I'm extinct!"

Something makes me look to Brokk, and he gives me the tiniest nod of encouragement.

"The king caught me on the night of the Hunt of the Moons," I continue. The people want more information, and Hunter sure isn't going to give it to them. "It was an omen." I'm repeating what Sian told me, but what else can I say when I don't even know the answers myself?

"An omen!" Now the people are chanting, repeating my words. Fuck, this is freaking me out. Again, I glance to Hunter for help. Again, he looks away. Goddamnit.

My empathy for his extreme discomfort in this situation is being severely tested on account of my *own* fucking extreme discomfort in this situation. *Please, help me.*

A soft vibration rolls through me. Hunter is purring. He brings my hand to his mouth and presses a kiss on the back. "Mine," he announces to the crowd. A couple villagers nudge each other with knowing smiles. A few women look like they're going to swoon.

Hunter and I share a look, and my heart gives a little lurch of hope. Maybe we *have* got this. Together.

The naked desire mixed with admiration in his bronze-flecked eyes sends warmth through my entire body, and I turn back to face the crowd with a little more courage. His hand finds mine, his broad thumb rubbing circles in my palm.

That, combined with another heady waft of his scent, reminds me of what his thumb feels like in other places on my body, and I swallow hard, pushing the naughty thoughts away.

Concentrate, girl, I tell myself. *You've got a kingdom to help run.*

And that's not a sentence I ever thought I'd hear myself think...

"Next petitioner?" Brokk calls out.

A group of worn-looking people in dusty clothes shuffle forward. The other better dressed villagers and courtiers give them wide berth. A soft growl rumbles deep in Hunter's chest, too low for anyone but me to hear. He scoots to the edge of the throne, like he's going to leap out at any moment. I'm not sure why. These people don't look like threats. They look in need of a bath, new clothes, and a good meal.

A sour scent rises from the battered group. I swallow against my nausea.

The foremost petitioner is a white-skinned male in a grey-green tunic the color of mold. He releases the hand of a small, white-skinned child, and steps forward. "Please, your Majesty. We are refugees from the Stone Kingdom. We've come to beg your intervention in our country."

Hunter's stopped growling. He's completely silent.

"Our country is ruined," the refugee continues. "We are starving. There is no food, no more forest. The land is parched. It has become a desert. The king forces us to work in the mines. Even our children are enslaved—"

A Beta male in a purple robe steps forward. "Enough. We cannot intervene. The Stone Kingdom belongs to the king, to do with as he pleases." He runs a hand down his beard. "Your kingdom is of the Stone King. His domain. To infringe upon it would be an act of war."

"He is a usurper. We are the rightful occupants of the land. Have you forgotten how he attacked your kingdom?"

"That was never proven," the councilor says, and turns

his back on the refugee. "There must be peace between our kingdoms for ours to thrive," he announces to us.

A new growl rumbles in Hunter's chest, like rich, rolling thunder.

Everyone in the room freezes.

I bite my lip. What am I supposed to say?

"Councilor Mikkan," Brokk says, but the purple-robed courtier waves him off.

"Please." The refugee ignores them both and steps closer to the throne, appealing straight to us. "The Stone King's greed knows no bounds. Soon he will no longer be content with sucking the life out of his own country, and will come for yours. It is only a matter of time!"

The room erupts in protest. "Hear, hear," someone shouts in the back, but several more villagers respond with cries of, "Nay!" Near the throne, rows of councilors murmur to each other. In the center of the hubbub, the grey-green garbed refugees stand quiet. The wan, deathly pale faces of the children are breaking my heart.

Someone jostles the refugee speaker, and Brokk steps in to protect him.

Hunter rises.

"My king." Mikkan turns, his hands raised. His smooth voice carries well, and the people around him fall silent. He's the one I heard outside the door—he summoned us to the audience. "You know that intervention is an impossibility. We cannot risk offending the Stone King." He signals to several Alpha guards. "Remove these troublemakers from the palace."

"No!" I want to shout, but it comes out a whisper. The noise of the crowd crashes over me. My chest seizes. I slump over, dizzy. I'm teetering on the edge of the throne when Hunter whirls, scoops me up, and strides from the audience chamber.

THIRTEEN

The Hunter King

AFTER ONE DAY in the palace—and the royal audience —I wish to leave and never return. Even Brokk's voice grates on me and makes my head ache. I take my little lysia flower back to the forest for a short while.

I want to be alone with her.

I had the Betas put together some food in a basket, and saddle up my tyrlee for us to ride. For a moment, I considered giving my new mate her own tyrlee but decided against it. I enjoy having her pressed up against me, cradled in my arms, her scent making my senses tingle.

As we ride to a favorite spot of mine—a deep, secluded pond, rich with wildlife—I mull over my Omega's adjustment to the palace so far, and to Arboron in general. She did well earlier, handling the audience we were forced to endure. It went well until the end. The Arborii seem to be delighted to have her as their new queen.

She is perfect, in every way.

And yet, she is unhappy; I can sense it in our bond.

When I rescued her from the royal audience, she asked me, "Why can't we help those people?"

I didn't respond. The truth is, I don't know. For as long as I've been king, the councilors have advised keeping peace with our border kingdoms. If I were more skilled with words, if I could explain that the Slythin are somehow bound to the Stone King by his cursed magic—maybe I could convince people of the threat. But I did not know how to make even Brokk understand. People believe what they wish to believe, and they block their ears to anything else. Why should I struggle to find the words when no one is listening?

It is easy to refuse to speak to the councilors. It is harder to refuse my Omega. She hasn't said much to me since the royal audience. Nor has she said a single word since we set off, which is unlike her.

My chest throbs. I ache to talk to her, to confide in her, but I cannot find the words. I don't know where to start. This—feeling this close to another—is so new to me, and I'm still trying to adjust. I never thought it would happen to me.

I thought Omegas were as good as extinct, and even when Khan and Aurus found a way to bring them here, I assumed they would do everything in their power to protect their new acquisitions.

Yet, here we are. I'm sitting astride a tyrlee with my very own Omega queen within my arms.

I throw back my head. I hate crowds, but this is one moment I wouldn't mind all my kingdom seeing. While I've always preferred my own company and solitude, Ulf has seen fit to grant me a companion—and she is everything I could have wished for.

My Haley.

We have reached the clearing, and I slide off the tyrlee before helping my mate dismount. The tyrlee is tied loosely to a tree, and I start setting up. I throw a fur on the grass and open the basket to see what the servants have given us.

"It's beautiful here." My lysia flower speaks at last, and a little thrill of pleasure goes through me at the sound of her voice. "Are we having a picnic?"

I nod and continue setting up, laying out fruit, bread, cheeses, and the potent, spicy wine everyone drinks at court. The suns are beginning their descent over the hills in the distance. The heat of the day will disappear with them. Perfect. We'll eat, and then we'll head back to the palace. To bed.

Haley is wearing a tunic once more, and supple knee-length boots to protect her feet out here in the forest. While she looked exquisitely regal and just stunning in the dress I had made for her, it's not a practical garment for riding, or for being outdoors. Most Arborii fashions are not practical, especially the designs for females. Which is why I refuse to wear the ceremonial robes the counselors insist on. Even Brokk sided against me, saying he understood, but I'd be a laughing stock in my usual leather breeches and vest. That the people would call me a barbarian king.

He was right. They do call me a barbarian. But I will never wear the ceremonial robes, or carry the clumsy, badly weighted ceremonial sword and scepter.

In her jeweled tunic, Haley looks more like a ruler than I'll ever be. Does she see me as a barbarian, the Wild One, as my people do?

Admiring her bare thighs, I feel myself getting hard again. The barbarian in me wants to tear her tunic in two, and let the folds fall away from her bare body. I could have her naked under me in half a blink.

But that will not convince her I am not a barbarian.

There was one time I spoke and everyone could understand. It was moon-cycles ago, at the King's Council, the first time I scented the sweetest perfume of a mythical creature. An Omega. I made myself heard because I had to. I had one chance to question, and see if I could find an Omega for myself.

And now she is here, a gift from Ulf. I have only to keep her.

Brokk is good with females. He speaks many flattering words. I will try them on her.

"Pretty," I say and reach out to pet her hair. My big hand is clumsy against her small head.

Haley's long eyelashes flutter. She touches her hair. "Oh, do you like my braid?"

"Yes." I don't know what else to say. My Omega is as beautiful as a sunrise, as nightfall when the moon flowers are in bloom. Her perfume rises, and my cock responds. I do not have the words to tell her what she means to me but I can show her. I scoot closer to her, ready to claim her lips and lay her out on the ground.

She turns her head. "Hunter? Are we going to eat?"

Right. Food. After we've eaten, maybe I'll rut her again right here, on the fur, in the glow of the setting suns.

At the thought of her beautiful face contorted with pleasure, the breathy gasps she gives when I'm bringing her to climax, I'm tempted to do it now, but then she spots the food I've laid out.

"Oh good, I'm starving." Settling herself cross-legged on the fur, she begins to sample the various dishes, breaking off a piece of bread and nibbling it before helping herself to some leeberries.

I should say something to her. Anything. But when I open my mouth, the words are stuck.

Once, when I was young, an older female in the village tried to take me in. She was alone and without children. She lured me in with roasted grain and the warm stones of her

105

hearth fire. I had been lurking around the village for so long, trying to act like a villager. Someone had tossed out a flea-ridden fur robe, and I wore that.

The woman chained me up in her yard. She'd hold food out, close to my hand, but not close enough to grab, and shout at me in the language I did not understand. I had to respond in her language, or she would toss the food into the dirt, too far away to reach. Sometimes, I repeated what she said and she was pleased. Those nights, I got to eat. Other nights—

"Hunter? Are you okay?" Haley wrinkles her forehead. She rubs her chest. My side of the bond is a roiling tempest of raw emotion. I must remember she can feel what I feel.

I grunt and touch her brow, tracing the soft skin until I've smoothed down her worry lines. I do not want to cause her distress.

I busy myself with the wine, pouring her a cup and handing it to her. She takes a sip, then screws her face up in a way that's hilarious and adorable. "Jesus, what is that?" she says. "It tastes like balsamic vinegar! That's gone stale in a shoe!"

I grunt and pull it away from her. My courtiers say the wine is an acquired taste, and I can't say I've acquired it.

Haley is still grimacing and wiping her mouth. "Is there anything else?"

I shake my head and get to my feet. She likes the drural fruits well enough. I can find some of those for her to drink from. I hold out a hand to stop her from rising to her feet, and point to the blankets.

"Stay here." She nods. "Got it."

I head off into the trees.

I've just found a drural tree when I hear a cry, and pain spikes through my heart. I whirl. Ahead, the bushes quiver and the tyrlee we rode here on crashes through the thorn bush, tossing her head and squealing, her eyes rolling and flashing white. Her torn lead hangs from her neck. I leap out of her way, letting her rush past. She brings with her a cold, gray scent, tinged with the scent of decay and mildew, mold and old bones. I know this stench well.

Overhead, birds are rising from the trees, squawking and calling, flying fast to escape. Like the tyrlee, they sense death has come to the forest.

A bitter, chalky taste fills my mouth. I tear through a thorn bush to return to Haley faster.

She's on her feet, motionless, staring at the Slythin which has reared up in a typical attack posture. It's within striking distance. A cold shard of dread pierces my chest.

The Slythin's eyes are black. A flakey gray substance coats its scales. It acts as an enamel, hardening the scales to armor. Slythin are generally not easy to kill, and this enamel makes it impossible.

Panic screams through the bond. Haley's eyes flash as white as the tyrlee's.

I hold out a hand, signaling her to be quiet. The movement should draw the Slythin's attention, and for a moment, it does. The cold eyes flick to me, but all too soon they refocus on Haley. I try desperately to connect with the creature but its mind is an impenetrable wall.

I will need a weapon for this. I race forward and rip a young sapling out of the ground, tearing it out at the roots as I rush towards the snake. Vines from the closest cex trees snap out to restrain the Slythin. It writhes, thrashing to get free of the vines. While it's distracted, I push Haley out of the way and thrust the root end of the sapling in its face. Dirt rains down as I beat it back.

The Slythin rears up, retreating from my clumsy attack. It opens its jaws. Fangs flash over my head. A bead of bright red poison drips from one fang. I leap out of the way and the acid venom drops to sizzle on the ground. It burns through the fallen twigs and leaves, not a fist length from my boot.

I'm used to fighting, to adrenaline coursing through my blood, but this time, it's different. A gut-churning, cold fear also fills me, threatening to hinder my fighting ability. It's not fear for myself. Haley is my everything. I would not survive losing her.

So I will protect her no matter what, even if it costs me my life.

FOURTEEN

Haley

OH MY GOD. Hands over my mouth, I back away, and trip over a cluster of rocks. My stupid tunic rips as I throw myself behind the biggest boulder.

The thing just came out of nowhere. Its coiled body wound silently through the brush until it reached me.

One snap of its jaws, and it could swallow a motorcycle whole.

The scent of mildew fills the air. Saliva pools in my mouth like I'm about to barf. I swallow hard.

The huge gray snake has tiny shriveled wings on its back. If that thing could fly, it would be terrifying. It's already terrifying.

Its head lunges forward again and again, mouth snapping. Hunter is wielding a small tree like a club. The snake bites the weapon and tosses it aside. In a blur of movement, Hunter leaps into the creature's mouth.

"No!" I'm on my feet behind the boulder, screaming. My nails bite into my palms. Somehow, Hunter emerges, leaping out of the thing's mouth with a white fang in his fist.

Venom rains down in a red curtain. Hunter ducks and weaves, dancing out of the way.

He's still holding the fang, a bone-white, massive needle that looks like the one mounted in the throne room. What did Sian call that creature? A Slythin? If this is a Slythin, then Hunter's beaten one before. This thing's fang isn't as big as the one in the throne room. It's smaller. Maybe it's a baby? Isn't a baby viper's poison more deadly than an adult's? Or is that a myth?

Hunter is running circles around the Slythin, but it twists and turns easily on its sliding coils. Its tail swishes over what looks like a puddle of acid, and the waxy scales smoke where the poison touches them, but the thing doesn't seem to care.

Hunter's running straight for a puddle of sizzling acid.

"Look out," I scream. Vines snap down from a nearby tree and Hunter grabs hold of them, letting them lift him as he swings above the puddles, Tarzan style.

I feel like an idiot, standing here, wringing my hands. What can I do? I don't remember my resume, but I'm pretty sure big-ass alien snakes aren't my forte. I'm completely worthless in this fight.

Hunter has drawn the creature away from the pools of acid. Now he's hanging on the snake's back, inching up the scales as the snake rears back and forth, plunging its head up and down while its tail undulates with breathtaking speed, trying to shake him off. Flecks of white are flaking off the gray scales, almost as if the snake is molting, or if it's sick or something. The rotting smell intensifies. I gag.

The snake whips its head around and tosses Hunter into the trees. The vines fly out to catch him, but miss.

The snake snaps around to face me.

Fuck!

I lift my form-fitting tunic and duck into the thicket.

Thorns tear at my skin, but maybe they'll slow the snake down. Or not, because its scales seem impenetrable.

I flail and skid on the leaves, pounding through the forest, twisting and turning, with branches whipping my face. I haven't run this fast since Hunter caught me. Maybe this is a sign I should take up marathoning.

The snake smashes through the thicket, crushing bushes under its scaly bulk. It rears up over me, pink maw open. A roar crescendos, shaking the trees. Hunter comes flying out of the forest, sailing in on a vine. The vine whips in an arc, sending him hurtling towards the snake's head. Hunter slams into the beast's head, clutching the fang like a spear. He drives it into the snake's eye.

The snake goes nuts, writhing in what I hope are death throes. The scaly coils uproot bushes, cracking trunks and ripping saplings out at the root. I throw myself behind a log, my arms over my head.

The forest falls silent.

My legs are too wobbly to move. I peek over the log. Hunter is standing over the felled snake. The fang is still sticking out of its right eye. Its remaining fang oozes venom that hisses when it splatters on the grass. The creature's coils stop twitching, and it lies still in the wreckage of the forest. The rotting smell dies away.

Hunter paces around the snake, running his hands over its still body. The grayish white film covering the scales sloughs off under his palm. The papery external shell falls away, revealing the brilliant red scales underneath.

Carefully, Hunter kneels at the creature's wedge-shaped head, avoiding the pooling acid. A vine creeps from a nearby tree. A wide leaf unfurls from its tip. Hunter snaps the leaf off carefully, and uses it to cover the snake's left eye. He bows his head.

Something twists in my heart. Hunter's gentle movements remind me of when he saved the baby creature I thought was attacking me. He treats the creatures of the forest with respect. Even the ones who try to kill us.

"Hunter." I hate how my voice is quavery, but my insides are still shaking. I need to touch him, to reassure myself we've both survived.

He rises, and rushes over. His hands cup my head as he looks me over.

"Hey," I whisper. My lower lip wobbles.

He scoops me up and I curl into him. His chest rumbles in a purr as he plunges into the forest, leaving the scene of destruction behind. I press my face into the crook of his neck and inhale his woodsy scent. I rub a cheek over his shimmery tattooed skin like I'm trying to bathe in him.

Hunter carries me to a fern grove. The giant fronds part as he passes. The air here is rich with loam and a piney, rosemary-like herbal scent.

"Should we get back to the palace?" I don't want any more snakes to burst out of the trees.

Hunter grunts, and I hear a whole paragraph of explanation in the guttural sound. The forest is quiet, calm. The air, warm and clean. No more of the rotting scent that preceded the Slythin.

Here, in the woods, Hunter is in his element. He prefers the forest to the palace. I'm not sure I don't, either.

He lays me down on a soft pile of leaves.

"It's okay," I gasp, grabbing his large hands as they roam over me. I need his skin on mine. "I'm not hurt. It didn't hurt me."

Hunter brushes a heavy hand over my head, easing me back.

"Show," he grunts. The end of the word turns into a growl that reverberates through me. My spine goes loose. I lie back, shaking. The torn hem of my tunic rides up.

Hunter kneels between my legs, pushing the tunic up the rest of the way. There are thorns sticking into the folds; he plucks them away and tosses them aside. He's gentle as he brushes my hair back from my face. His thumb doesn't touch my jaw but I wince anyway. There's a scrape there.

"It's okay," I whisper. "Just a scratch."

He curls his blunt fingers into the neck of my tunic, and rips it clean in half. I start at the ripping sound but he's tossed the folds back, baring me to his gaze. A pleasing shudder runs through my lower half.

Hunter stretches out over me, careful not to let his giant frame rest on mine. He nuzzles at my shoulder where a red scrape blooms on my skin. His lips brush the unharmed skin above the scrape. At his butterfly light touch, every muscle between my legs contracts with a sharp, delicious clench. I curl into him with a whimper, unable to rub myself against him because he's pinning me down. He runs his nose down my neck, leaving goosebumps in its wake. So careful, so gentle. Taking his sweet time.

When I close my eyes, I see the snake rising up over me again. My breath shudders out of me.

Hunter digs his fingers into my hair, cradling my head, chafing my face with his beard until I open my eyes.

I stroke the furrows in his brow. "That thing was huge. You could've died."

"No." He doesn't sound arrogant. He sounds sad.

"I'm sorry I wasn't more help," I say. "I looked for a dagger or something to fight with but..." My fighting skills are about as good as his talking ones.

"No," Hunter says again. His growl vibrates through me, making me throb again. Slick pools hotly between my legs.

"You saved me," I whisper.

He turns his head and kisses my palm. So sweet. He

113

draws my fingers into his mouth, sucking hard. My clit throbs as if he laid his mouth on me.

"I'm okay," I gasp, as he turns his attention to a scratch on my collarbone. I grab his head to pull him away. "You don't need—"

He pins my wrists to the ground with a growl. My hips judder as a new spurt of slick soaks my core.

Vines creep across the ground, winding about my wrists and ankles to tether me in place. I'm spread-eagled, and open to Hunter's ministrations. He kisses his way down my chest, pausing at a red mark on my hip. He bends and peppers kisses around the mark. More slick trickles out of me. My perfume blooms on the air. The combination of Hunter's scent and mine makes my eyelids flutter.

I fight the vines, thrashing to press closer to him. I spread my thighs wide, lifting my hips to find his. "Hunter, I need…"

He rears over me, unfastening his breeches enough to let his cock spring out then lowering his hips to weight mine. Another growl triggers a sharp throb, and a gush of slick. He pushes inside, rocking back and forth until his shaft is fully inside, filling me to the brim.

The vines holding my arms snap, releasing me. I claw at his back as we shudder and rock together. I need him closer. I need more. When he pins me down and drives his cock into me with hard, punishing thrusts, my orgasm explodes. Pleasure sears my limbs. Hunter growls again and again, pulling wave after wave of sensation through my body. My inner muscles ripple, clenching down on his cock. The ferns around us shake and rustle with his roar. His fangs nip my bare shoulder, awakening a memory of the first time he bit me. Warmth pours through my body as my climax swells and breaks in a continuous, undulating tide.

The force of my roar echoes around the grove. Haley's as tight as a clenched fist. A few more rocking thrusts, and then I graze her shoulder with my teeth and release the pleasure burning up my back. My knot fills my Omega's perfect pussy, pulsing in time with my thundering heartbeat.

Twilight has settled over the forest. The first moon has climbed above the trees, soon to be joined by her sisters.

The fern fronds dance in the breeze. I lie over my little lysia flower, sheltering her from the cooling air, letting my seed and her slick seal us together. Her eyes are half closed, her lashes tiny shadows on her face.

I kiss her smooth cheek and nuzzle her neck. Her eyes blink open.

"A fern grove wouldn't be my first choice for a good place to hook up, but it's kind of perfect." Her fingers run over my face, finding my scars and tracing them as if reassuring herself that I'm here. They falter, and I nudge her hand until she keeps touching me.

A line appears between her brows. "What was that thing? she asks. "Was that a Slythin? Sian told me about them."

I nod.

"Are they from the forest?"

I shake my head.

"Then where do they come from?"

I could answer her. I have my suspicions. The whitish film coating the Slythin's scales reeked of magic. The creatures are desert dwellers, and only one kingdom we share a border with has a large desert—the Stone Kingdom, ruled

115

by the Stone King. I don't trust any of the kings of Ulfaria, but the Stone King is the one I trust the least. If that venomous usurper thinks he's getting his filthy, cracked talons on my Omega, I will show him why the courtiers still call me *feral* behind my back.

Haley flinches. I'm growling, canines bared. I smooth her hair in apology, but she angles her head, averting her gaze from mine. I cup her cheeks, ready to force her to look at me, but can only hold her.

"Never mind," she whispers. "I'll ask Sian to tell me."

I want her to speak to me. I want her to understand. I want to tell her to look at me, tell her to call me by my name. Not the name she's given me, but the name I'm slowly starting to remember because of the memories she's unlocked for me.

I nuzzle her. I'm still deep inside her body, but she could not be more far away.

How do I explain I want to talk to her but my words are stiff and clumsy, more like an animal's howl than pretty speech?

If I say the wrong thing, I will lose her. She will hate me. The villagers drove me away with sticks and stones. The only reason the Arborii accepted me is because I killed so many Slythin. Spears and swords glance off their scaly hides, which makes them the perfect hunters.

I have more in common with the Slythin than my own people.

"It's getting late," Haley says. I shift inside her, easing my way from her body. When I have withdrawn, an ache spreads through my chest. A melancholy echo throbs in the bond.

I bow my head and capture her lips, sweeping my tongue inside her mouth. Tasting, conquering. Bringing her back to me. The sadness disappears, driven out by heat.

But I cannot kiss her forever. When I'm done, Haley lays a palm against my cheek. She worries her bottom lip with her small teeth, more lines appearing above her brows.

"We should get back to the palace," is all she says.

I nod and lift her into my arms. The yaknos ferns reach out to brush me as I pass, as if their subtle caress might give me comfort. But I am like a dying tree—standing tall, but barren, hollow inside.

I need to find the words to woo her, to make her feel close to me. I could lose her if I use them clumsily. But I am losing her now.

FIFTEEN

The Hunter King

FOUR OF THE five moons have risen by the time I step onto the expanse of shorn grass outside the palace. Night insects creak and sing, glowing red. My Omega is bundled in my arms, wrapped in the tatters of her beautiful garment. Our hair is full of leaves, our boots muddied. I am every inch the barbarian returning from a ruined outing with his mate.

I hoped to slink into the palace without anyone noticing, but a group of courtiers have ordered a fire built in the stone pit on the palace lawn. Firelight plays on their laughing faces. They are wearing their long, ornate robes and drinking bitter wine.

For a moment, I am once again the outcast on the edge of the fire. But Haley sighs—she's half asleep, and her bare limbs are chilled by the night air. I spur my steps on.

The bell tolls, announcing my arrival. The courtiers look around and rise in clumsy waves when they see us. I ignore them and their greetings, but Mikkan appears at my side.

"Your Majesty, what has happened?"

"Slythin," I grunt, and speed up my stride. For once, I am grateful for the palace, the sturdy structure, and the layers of defenses that will keep my mate safe.

"I knew it. The creatures are back, and they will not stop coming until they've driven us out of hearth and home!" Mikkan trots along beside me, wringing his hands together. His fear has a sour scent.

I reach the steps of the palace and take them two at a time.

Brokk emerges from the palace, takes one look at me, and sends the courtier scurrying. "Not now, Mikkan. Send for food, and water for a bath."

I keep walking, Brokk falls into step behind me. I cannot tell him, but I appreciate his guard at my back while my arms are full of my mate. The Alpha guards are generally good security, but I don't trust all of them.

"Any injuries?" Brokk asks.

I shake my head.

"What happened? A Slythin attack?"

I nod. I've reached the hall to our quarters. Brokk strides ahead to open the door.

"See to your mate. We'll talk later."

I duck inside, carrying Haley straight to the tub. She likes to be clean. The servants have already drawn a hot bath, and I set her down to strip off her boots and the torn remains of her tunic. She grips my hand as she steps in, hissing as her feet hit the water.

I back up, leaving muddy bootprints on the floor. I do not belong here. In the forest, I'm at ease. Here, the air closes in, stealing my breath. Footsteps echo in the stone halls, stealing my peace. The assorted smells are too strong and concentrated.

"Hunter?" Haley's cheeks are flushed. She's melted

against the side of the tub but stretches her fingers towards me. "Do you want to wash?"

I grab a cloth and dunk it in the bath, running it over the muddiest parts of myself. If I stare too long at my Omega's body in the water, I'm going to want to rut her again.

My cock swells. Maybe I should—

Water sloshes and by the time I turn, Haley has exited the bath. She's wrapped a cloth around herself but plenty of her light golden skin is on display, wet and gleaming.

"What's wrong?" She pulls the sodden mass of her dark hair into a bunch and leans over the bath to squeeze the water from it. It'd be so easy to whip her around and bend her over the tub, but... no. She wants to talk.

She always wants to talk, and I have no words for her.

"You don't blame yourself for the attack?" she asks.

I shrug. A king protects his kingdom. His people. Above all, his Omega.

I stomp away from the tub ahead of her, and snatch up a tunic the servants have laid out for her.

Haley follows. The bond between us is heavy, as if laden with river silt. She takes the tunic and turns away, murmuring to herself, "I wish I could understand you."

She thinks she's spoken too low for me to hear, but I did hear her. Without thinking, I stride to the outer wall, where large windows display the forest. Every other panel can swing outward. One is cracked open to let the night air in. It would be so easy to run.

She wants me to make myself known to her. What would I say? I barely remember a few things about my parents. I remember the warmth of my mother, followed by fear and loss. My mother and my father are dead, I am sure of it, but I don't remember how. The forest became my home. I learned the language of the vines and trees before I learned to speak. I grew curious of my fellow Ulfarri, but the villagers threw stones, and I learned to stay away.

I should have stayed in the forest.

A small hand is placed in the center of my back. I still. Haley sidles up to me and presses herself against my back. Her hand makes its way around until she's splayed it over my chest. Despite the sullen, black echo in the bond between us, I capture her hand and press it to my heart.

"It's not your fault, Hunter." Her breath puffs between my shoulder blades. "You saved us. You saved me."

I thread my large fingers between her tiny ones. She is closer to me than any other. Maybe I can make her understand.

Boots scuffle outside the door, preceded by a sour scent. My head snaps in that direction just before a sharp rap rings out on the wood.

"My king," comes Mikkan's muffled voice. "Please. There is an emergency in the throne room. You must come and see."

Haley

We're back in the audience chamber again. It's only been a short while since that hideous giant snake reared up, but instead of going to bed and being held by Hunter, which is what I want—*need*—to do, we need to face the angry mob demanding that the king do something about the Slythin.

Having seen them up close and personal, I can understand that now, more than ever. I've never been afraid of snakes, but fuck, that one was bigger than a car. It could have fit my entire body into its mouth.

I shudder.

Hunter was heroic and sexy in the way he rescued me, and once again I'm struck by the contrast between what he says and what he does. He's hard to read and he struggles to communicate—probably because of delayed speech development—but he treats me so well... organizing a romantic picnic, rescuing me from a monster, looking at me like I'm the most precious thing in the world to him.

Now he's on the throne beside me, glaring down the agitated mob. I didn't even get a chance to grab a different tunic, which is why I've got my legs crossed firmly while I'm sitting on this throne. The tunic only goes to mid-thigh, I don't want to give the Arborii an eyeful of my lady parts.

The mob in the chamber is settling. Angry mutters are more muted. A few villagers have brought their children, and in the back of the room, a baby is crying. The sound sets my teeth on edge.

It's like they're afraid.

The group of councilors, who hang around Hunter like a flock of crows whenever we're here at the palace, stand to the left of us. Mikkan is in the center of the cluster. The hood of his purple robe is pushed back and he's stroking his long, wispy beard.

Brokk appears and climbs up the dais to whisper something in Hunter's ear.

Hunter's green brows snap together. His jaw clenches, his whole body goes rigid. He glances at me before giving a curt nod.

A hooded Beta appears on the right, walking with his hands outstretched. In front of his hands hovers a glowing orb bigger than my head. He walks to the center of the room and squares off to the throne, leaving the ball floating in midair in front of us.

The magician's ball seems to be filled with a white mist. Everyone is staring at it like it's the second coming.

I glance at Hunter, wishing that he'd take my hand. I'm nervous, and I can't even say why. The globe pulses with a grey-white light, and everyone flinches. Everyone except Hunter. I lean over towards him, but he doesn't notice.

The fog inside the globe clears, and a figure appears. They're wearing a deep hood, but the hands clasped in front of them are pale and covered in bulging blue veins, with sharp-tipped nails that are horribly long, like misshapen claws. Glowing, pinkish eyes burn from within the shadow of the hood.

"Hunter King. Greetingsss. It ssseems you have sssome-thing of mine," they say. They hiss on the consonants, and a shudder goes up my spine. This is creepy as hell.

Hunter grunts. If ever there was a time for him to say something, it would be now. But he only angles his head towards Brokk. The big Alpha steps forward and lets his voice ring out.

"Greetings, Stone King. What is it you are looking for?"

Hunter's face is blank, but he's leaning forward, his muscles bunched and tense. I'm squeezing my hands together so hard that I'm hurting myself. I force myself to loosen them a bit. So this is the Stone King. Even more awful than I imagined.

"The Omega," the terrifying king says, and all eyes in the room swivel to land on me. I wish I could sink through the seat of the chair and just disappear.

Hunter is the only one who does not look my way. I'm squeezing my fingers again. All his attention is fixed on the floating screen. He's one hundred percent focused, like he was when he faced down the giant snake.

"She isss mine," the Stone King continues when he real-izes he's not getting an answer. "I commissioned an...

associate... to use the Ogsul technology. Why should Aurus and Khan be the only ones to have an Omega by their sssides? All went well at first, and they were indeed able to bring a Hoo-man to Ulfaria. Unfortunately, I'm working with incompetent dolts, and during the delivery they configured sssomething wrong—" here, he waves a talon-tipped hand dismissively, "—long ssstory short, she ended up in Arboron and not *my* kingdom. Here. With *me*. I want her returned."

I glance at Hunter. There's a muscle ticking in his jaw and it looks like he's considering it.

Surely not.

"If you do not return her, I will unleash the Slythin army upon your kingdom."

A murmur goes around the room. The Stone King has confirmed he's responsible for the Slythin.

"The creatures will overrun your borders. Kill your children. Ruin your crops. Surely she isss not worth that?" the creepy Stone King says.

The murmurs continue, but Hunter is silent.

"The Hunter King has done so much for his people," Brokk says, his deep, rumbling voice a stark contrast to the slimy, hissing tones of the Stone King. "Surely he deserves an Omega of his own? Besides, he has claimed her. They are bonded."

There's a strange hiccupping sound, accompanied by wheezes. The Stone King is laughing. Kind of. "She is not Ulfarri. Claiming has no meaning the way it did in the old days. I can ssstill possess her."

"Wait a minute," I say, "I'm not some object to be passed around!"

Brokk's eyes flick to me, then back to the screen. He is the only one who even acknowledges that I said anything.

The people are silent. The councilors are all staring at their feet.

I look at Hunter, who's doing a great impression of Rodin's *The Thinker* right now. The only thing moving in his entire body is still that muscle in his jaw. He doesn't even acknowledge that I'm there. A wave of mixed emotions flows through me—despair, fear, frustration, but most of all, disappointment. I thought he cared about me. And here he is, actually considering the creepy creature's proposal? Considering *letting me go*?

"We ask for some time to consider it," Brokk says, breaking the long, awkward silence.

There's a pause. Then, "I have waited a long, long time for an Omega," the Stone King says. "I can wait one more day. You have until the sssuns set tomorrow. Then I will unleash the Slythin, and the Arborii—indeed, Arboron itself —will be decimated."

Hunter stands. The room falls silent. The rows of people closest to the throne look up at his face and step back. Goosebumps rise on my arms. There's a bright, burning feeling in the bond. I grit my teeth against the swelling ache under my ribs. I can't move.

With one stride, Hunter clears the steps and bounds up to the orb. When the servant brought the magician's ball in, they never touched the surface. Hunter fights through an invisible force-field surrounding the ball. His roar drowns out the cries from Brokk and Mikkan—

"No! You cannot!"

Hunter grabs the orb. Light blazes around his hands, bright enough to blind. I cry out, along with several members of the crowd. Hunter leaps into the air and raises his arms, spiking the orb. It smashes on the flagstones at his feet. There's another blast of light, and a chemical smell rises.

What the actual fuck?

The room erupts. People in the back scoop up their crying children. There's a stampede to leave. Alpha guards are shouting.

The hooded councilors and courtiers throng the throne, crowding as close to the dais as they can without getting near the broken orb that's oozing foul-smelling fluid onto the floor.

"This is an abomination," one is shouting. "You have given injury to the Stone King!"

"This could mean war!"

"There is only one answer," Mikkan says. "We must surrender the Omega to the Stone King." His eyes flit over me before he turns to the rest of the councilors, some of whom are nodding along. "She is rightfully his. He arranged —and likely paid a great deal—to have her brought here."

"He *stole* the Ogsul technology," Brokk argues, pushing through the crowd. "I doubt he paid anything. Besides, that is of no consequence. Surely after everything the Hunter King has done for our people, he deserves an Omega. He saved us from the Slythin once, he can do so again. You should be standing by him." He glares at the chaotic room. "*All* of you! We should support our king!"

I'm frozen on the throne. There's a deep, throbbing ache in my chest. Disheartened doesn't seem a good enough word for what I'm feeling. Devastated is more like it.

Hunter stands over the orb. He nudges a shard of glass with his foot, looking like he wishes it wasn't broken, so he can smash it again.

Unable to stand to look at him for a moment longer, I slide off my chair and rush out of the room. Nobody follows me.

He doesn't follow me.

I'm blinded by stinging tears but I don't know why I'm

weeping. My feet take me straight to our private quarters—when did I start regarding them as ours?— but I'm unable to get in on account of the stupid magic doors hidden within the wall.

I stand in front of them, glaring.

Luckily, a hooded Beta appears.

"Open them," I say, and my voice has a ringing command to it I didn't even know I was capable of.

The servant glides to a tile and as soon as she's standing on it, the thick doors slide smoothly open.

"Thank you. I do not wish to be disturbed." With as much dignity as someone who was just bested by a set of doors can muster, I march on into the bedchamber.

Then I throw myself onto the furs on the giant bed, squeeze my eyes shut to prevent the tears from coming, and try to gather my thoughts. I want to make a pillow fort out of all the cushions, but I'm too upset. The room is stuffy and strange. Without Hunter, it doesn't feel safe.

That's the second court audience that was a dumpster fire. This whole thing is insane. I'm on an alien planet, and I'm some special Omega who's so precious that I'm passed around like a Pokémon card?

What if the councilors get their way, and I'm given to the Stone King?

And Hunter smashing the orb—does this mean we're at war? What the fuck is going to happen now? If the councilors do get their way, what the fuck am I going to do?

The worst part is, I need Hunter more than ever, and things aren't right between us. Why am I so hurt by him? Who is he to me? It's not like I chose him. Like we went on dates and he wooed me. Like any of this went the way things usually go when two people discover they have feelings for each other. Like I even know his fucking name.

There's a grunt, and I look up to see him standing there. His hazel eyes sweep over me.

There's a tightness in my chest that makes it hard to breathe. This must be the bond Sian told me about. I don't know if what I'm feeling is from him or me. I feel despair... and rage. The desire to go kill the Stone King. That one's probably Hunter's.

"Hey-leah," he says, and even though he struggles to say it, my name on his tongue makes my belly flutter.

"Go away," I mutter. "I want to be alone."

Ignoring me, even though I know for a fact he heard me, he gets down on the bed with me and lays a huge, possessive hand on my ass.

His smoky, syrupy scent fills me and when his hand slides down to caress the back of my thigh before creeping between my legs, the sudden rush of liquid heat almost takes my breath away.

Goddamn it, why do I have to react to him this way? It's like my body has a mind of its own.

Any second now, he's going to pull me into his arms. He'll start purring. Then he'll growl. I'll get wet, and he'll rut and knot me and it'll feel good, but nothing will be fixed.

"No," I say, shaking him off before scrambling up off the furs. It takes every ounce of willpower I possess, but I manage it. "I don't want to fuck. That's not going to fix anything."

His face, when I dare to glance at him, is set in a wounded yet stubborn expression. Like a petulant child who's been told they can't have another cookie.

"I'm freaking out, Hunter. I need to know what's going on, and—" my throat clogs with tears, "I need you to talk to me. I know it's hard for you. I don't know what's going on and I'm so scared." I fold my arms around my middle, squeezing tight. If I squeeze hard enough, maybe I won't cry.

Hunter scoots closer to me and I back further away. "No. If you touch me, it's only going to lead to one thing and I just can't right now, Hunter. I can't." I double over. His scent is so thick, I can taste it. The pain in my chest is almost debilitating. "Can you please just go get Sian? I need to talk to someone."

My fight against tears isn't working. I blink as Hunter rises up off the bed with his usual feline grace. He takes a step towards me, his hand outstretched. Another wave of his scent rolls through me, making me ache for him. "Hey-leah."

A part of me relaxes. His hand closes on the nape of my neck, soothing me. I want to melt back against him. With a feeling like I'm tearing myself in two, I wrench myself away. "Get off me, you barbarian."

Hunter stands with his hand frozen in midair, his blank face at odds with the sting knifing through my chest.

"I'm sorry," I stutter, backing away. "I didn't mean... I just want to be alone." I rush into the bathing chamber—which, thank god, has a regular door. Slamming it shut behind me, I sink to the floor and put my face in my hands. Pain gnaws at my ribs. I can finally let the tears come.

My sobs echo around the bathing chamber. I cry and cry until I can't cry anymore. I didn't realize how much I was holding in, but it was obviously a lot. I'm on an alien planet, and I have no one to talk to. I care for someone whose name I don't even know, who doesn't seem to return my feelings. And tomorrow I might be given to that creepy Stone King—and if I don't go, he might declare war on a bunch of innocent people. Am I willing to sacrifice myself for a kingdom? Will I even have a choice?

I wish I had someone to talk to. If I could get away to see

the other humans; I'm sure it would help. Right now, though, the only other person I can think of who might be able to give me advice is Sian.

I don't know how long I was in the bathing room, but when I return to the bedchamber, it's empty.

Hunter has gone, just like I asked him to.

So why do I feel so hollow?

SIXTEEN

The Hunter King

SEEING the hurt on my little lysia flower's face made me feel like my chest was going to explode. To know I caused that hurt... I think death would be less painful.

And yet, when I wanted to explain, I couldn't.

How could I tell her that she means everything to me? That when the Stone King talked about taking her, I vowed, then and there, to rip his face off?

The Stone King. What a pathetic excuse for an Alpha. For a king. For an Ulfarri. I do not fear that wretched, hideous creature, or his snake army.

I protected the people of Arboron when I was barely grown. I will do it again, if necessary, and again, and again... until I breathe my last. No, the thought of a Slythin attack does not scare me.

But the thought of losing my Haley...

That is unbearable.

I could run, and keep her in the forest. Leave the kingdom to its own devices. But she would not like living in the wild.

Barbarian, she called me.

I must make things right. Remove the lines of sorrow from her beautiful face. I summoned Sian as she asked, and now I am standing vigil outside the palace.

Brokk finds me standing at a firepit, staring into the flames. The smoke swirls around me, clogging my senses. I heard but did not scent his approach.

My second-in-command squats near the fire. He produces a bottle of wine and a large horn. For once, I do not care about the taste that my Omega describes as vinegar steeped in old shoes. I toss back the horn Brokk hands me, and accept the bitter burn in my throat. Once it's empty, I return it to him and he fills it again.

Until I met my Omega, I never felt a true bond with another in the sense that they have become my world, my stars and my moons, but I have always had a true supporter in Brokk. He talks too much, but unlike the councilors who talk too much and say so little, his words have weight and meaning. He is one of the few I listen to.

"Let me guess," he says as soon as we're alone, "the queen is upset."

I nod, staring into the fire.

"Can you blame her? The Stone King's proposal has shaken all of us. Mikkan wants us to hand her over. Many of the councilors agree."

I growl.

"I'm with you," Brokk says. "Handing over your Omega is unthinkable. Besides, appeasing that creature is not the way to go." He sips at the horn, then rolls it between his palms, which he does when he is thinking. "As an Alpha, I know how deep the bond between you and your claimed mate runs. The same can't be said, however, for her. She is new to all this—to our world, our people, to the way we mate. She was not even an Omega before she arrived. How is she meant to understand how you feel about her?"

I close my eyes as each of his words hits home like a poisoned dart.

"She's new here, and alone. And hurting."

I grunt. Haley is not alone. I should be at her side. But she doesn't want me.

The wine scalds my throat when I swallow it.

"Do you want me to talk to her?" Brokk asks.

A wave of sudden possessive jealousy at the mere idea almost makes me physically shudder. "No," I manage. Would my little lysia flower not be better suited to an Alpha like Brokk? One who can express himself easily, share his thoughts, his laughter...

I push the thought down. It makes me ache too much.

"What are we going to do about that creepy fuck?" Brokk changes the subject. "The people are scared almost out of their minds, and it's understandable. We must protect them."

I nod.

"Do you want me to summon the fighters?"

Arboron does not have an official army, like Aurus or Khan do. We Arborii are peaceful, nature-loving people who prefer to stay out of territorial disagreements or fights. But we will defend ourselves and our home if necessary, and we have enough Alphas and strong Betas who have pledged themselves to step up whenever the need arises. They may not have fancy uniforms or rigid military training, but does that matter when lives are at stake?

I meet Brokk's eyes.

"Right. We should also make arrangements for those who will not be fighting to shelter somewhere safe. We can hold a couple hundred here in the palace. The others...

some have bunkers. Others will find caves. I'll send out instructions for the people to get ready."

I take the horn, drain it, and hand it back with a nod.

"Maybe I should be the king around here," Brokk grumbles and, despite my bad temper, I bite back a smile. We both know he'd be welcome to take my throne if he chose to.

Ulf knows, I do not want it. It was forced upon me as a 'reward' for defeating the Slythin all those moons ago. It was intended as a compliment, I know, but I always was so ill-suited to be king. I've often thought it a shame that Brokk can't be king. Then again, I don't know whether the Arborii would accept him taking on the role.

Brokk hooks the horn to his belt and rises. "How likely is it that we will be fighting the Slythin?" he asks. "I mean, I know you will not give up the queen, but are you planning to mount a defense, or are you going to ride into the forest and defeat them single-handedly again?"

I stroke my beard, pondering his question. There are secrets I have about the Slythin, secrets I have never told anyone. They were not always enslaved by the Stone King's magic. But how do I explain that to my people?

"Think on it," Brokk says. "I will have the Alpha fighters ready." His blue gaze is frank, earnest, trustworthy.

I clap him on the shoulder.

"Actually, while we're discussing tactics, I wanted to suggest something to you." He lowers his voice, as he always does when disclosing sensitive information, even if we are alone. "Your advisors—especially the chief one, Mikkan—"

A growl erupts from me, surprising us both.

"Exactly," Brokk says, leaning closer. "I find him to be more and more untrustworthy. There have been whispers that he has been behaving suspiciously. I don't know whether it would be better to dismiss him outright, or keep a closer eye on him while letting him remain so as not to make

134

him suspect he's being watched, but I believe you should do something."

"I will." I've never liked any of my councilors—always flapping around me and squawking at me like the world's most irritating birds—but I tolerate them since they do so much of the work I like least about ruling a kingdom: negotiating, paperwork, dealing with trivial complaints and disputes. Since I always saw them as a flock, one never stood out from the rest. They're all equally annoying, as far as I'm concerned.

"It might be nothing," Brokk continues, "but as I said, I've been hearing murmurs. Have you had any disagreements with Mikkan, or any of them?"

I consider the question. Nothing stands out. I sometimes openly show my exasperation with the advisors, but that has been the case for years.

I shake my head.

"Hmm. Well, just so long as you're aware."

I give him a grunt of appreciation. There's a deep, pounding ache in my skull and, when I tentatively probe my bond with my mate, there's a different kind of pain: a deep, unbearable sorrow. Are those her feelings, or mine? I close my eyes.

"Don't worry," Brokk says. "We'll work things out and defeat that fucker." He claps me on the shoulder. "Go back to your queen and comfort her. Explain everything. Ulf knows, if I were you, if I were lucky enough to have an Omega mate, I wouldn't leave her side for a second, and would do everything in my power to make her happy."

My fists are clenched so tight, my nails dig into my palms. I force my fingers to uncurl. Brokk has been obsessed with the idea of fated mates since we were young. Most Alphas have accepted the fact that there is a dearth of Omegas on Ulfaria, and that they will never go on to experi-

135

ence the rut, claiming, knotting and so on like their ancestors did. That they will never sire offspring. I myself had accepted it long ago.

But not Brokk. He has never given up hope, and now that there are three Omega queens here on our planet, he will no doubt only be more determined to find one of his own. If I could help him achieve that, I would. He deserves happiness.

"Soon," I say.

"Ah." He slaps my back. "To the drinking hall then. Your queen will be safe."

I follow him back into the palace. I wish to return to my lysia flower, but her words of rejection sting. I will give her the space she needs before I return to her. In the meantime, I will post more Alpha guards to make sure she is safe.

If anything ever happened to her...

I cannot even finish that thought.

SEVENTEEN

Haley

I'M PACING the room when there's a rap on the door. I've been going round and round, trying to figure the situation out, and I'm going mad. The Ulfarri-King sized bed and all the cute little pillows call to me, but I'm resisting.

Part of me wishes we'd never left the cave.

"My queen?" Sian calls, and pokes her head in. "You sent for me?"

"Come in." I sink into a chair. Hunter listened, and found Sian for me. Maybe he is capable of doing more than rutting me, and growling.

Sian's gaze is filled with concern when she arrives and spots my swollen eyes, red and sore from crying. "How are you?"

"I'm fine." I hug a cushion to myself.

"That is what people say when they are not." When she leans over me for a hug, I almost break down again. I release the pillow to hug her back.

"Things are so fucked up," I whisper. "And Hunter and I..." I squeeze my eyes shut.

"The king adores you," Sian says, releasing me and perching on a seat beside me.

Even as my brain calls her a liar, a ridiculous surge of hope floods my heart. "How can you be so sure? Were you at the audience just now?" I didn't see her there. My attention was elsewhere.

"I was."

"I don't know what to do. They think I'm some possession to be passed around without any regard to my fucking feelings..." my voice is rising but I'm past caring, "Hunter is no help. His councilors act like he's a big kid—and then he smashes that orb and makes things worse!" *And he wouldn't even look at me.*

"It'll be all right."

"Easy for you to say. No one's calling for you to be sacrificed to the Stone King." I shiver, and she tugs one of the furs towards me. I pull it around my shoulders gratefully.

"You're not going to be given to the Stone King—"

I tune her out, burrowing into soft fur. It smells like Hunter, and the forest.

Things were simpler in the forest. Too bad we couldn't stay there. Maybe I could just escape... go elsewhere, somehow. Find a way to get to one of the other humans.

The thought of leaving Hunter is like a dagger to my belly but I push the pain aside. He'd get over it. Sometimes it seems like he only wants me for my body.

"My queen?" Sian sits with her hands folded in her lap, waiting for me to pay attention again. "Why would you think we would appease that awful king?"

"You heard the advisors—"

"But, forgive me, I saw the king's face." She gives a little laugh. "You were beside him. I was in the crowd—perhaps more able to see his expression?" She asks it as if she's worried about offending me. After her accusatory questions in our last conversation, she settled down and we talked normally for the remainder. Maybe she just grilled me because she feels somehow protective over King McGreeny. "I saw his face," she continues gently. "In the beginning, he was forcing himself to remain calm because all he wanted to do was kill the Stone King for even suggesting such a thing."

"You think so?" I press three fingers to my chest, where an aching throb has hooked itself behind my breastbone.

"The king will never let you go," Sian says.

"I don't know what I'm doing here," I tell her. "I have no one to talk to besides you. Hunter—he won't talk to me, or communicate in any way. I know it's hard for him but..." I close my eyes. "I didn't ask for this. Maybe I should leave, and everything will be fine."

Sian sits up straighter. "The king would never allow that."

I rub at my chest. The swelling pressure under my ribs has increased, making my stomach roil. "I could slip away and hide."

"He's the Hunter King. He would find you."

"Yes, he would." The pressure in my chest releases. *Hunter would never let me go.* Is it fucked up that I'm relieved? I rub a hand over my face. "What the fuck am I going to do?"

Sian is about to respond when the door flies open, and Mikkan comes striding in. His eyes are wild and he's stroking his beard compulsively. He's flanked by two guards I don't recognize.

Sian leaps up. "What is the meaning of this?"

Mikkan points to me. "Seize her."

I jump up but it's too late—the guards grab me, one to each arm, yanking me out from under the fur. I'm struggling with all my might, trying to shake them off. They're Betas, but they're still much stronger than I am.

"Let her go!" Sian steps in front of me, but Mikkan waves a hand and she stops. Her eyes go weirdly unfocused. Is there some kind of magic afoot? There's magic on this planet: what Hunter did with the vines was proof enough of that.

"When the king hears of this—" I begin, but I'm interrupted by a deafening crunch, followed by a hissing that makes my blood run cold. It's like the noise the Slythin made in the forest, but a million times louder.

A gigantic snake—at least five times the size of the one we encountered earlier—has burst through the wall of windows.

The freaking windows!

It fixes me with one cold, calculating eye. Its scales are ghostly pale. It has one enormous, glistening fang.

One fang that happens to be the exact same size as the one currently mounted in the audience chamber. It's not dripping venom—small mercies—but it's bigger than I am.

Is this the snake Hunter fought all that time ago? It's still alive?

"Put her in the cage!" the councilor snaps. "He'll be back at any moment!"

"And what do you think the king will do to you when he returns to find me gone?" I find my voice. The guards are dragging me over to the hissing, spitting creature. My boots scrape over the ground, crunching the broken glass. "He'll kill you before you can blink!"

"He won't know it was me." Mikkan fists his beard. "Do you think I'm that stupid?"

"Sure looks that way," I mutter, then scream as one of the guards lets go of me to open the door to a metal cage which is strapped around the Slythin's neck.

Is this fucking happening?

The cage's hinges creak so bad, they hurt my ears. It's

coated in some sort of white flaking stuff that stinks like mold.

Why, oh why did I send Hunter away? The bond pinches in my chest. I probe it, trying to communicate with him. *Please come*, I beg silently, frantically. *Please come and rescue me.*

There's no reply. All I feel is panic.

"Why are you doing this?" I ask as the guards shove me into the cage. The bars are cold and slimy against my bare legs. I'm still in the fucking short tunic. I'm shaking violently. I force myself to maintain the conversation. Maybe I can still persuade this asshole to relent. "The king is considering giving me up."

The bearded advisor gives a short, unpleasant bark of laughter. "He is not! He claimed you. He is an Alpha. You are his Omega. He would die for you. He would burn the kingdom to the ground before he gave you up. I, on the other hand, must consider the needs of Arboron. Of the Arborii people."

"The *king* is considering the needs of his people! Didn't he save them once before?" First Sian, now this guy. Both seem dead certain that Hunter would never send me away.

"That was before he had a mate. You do not understand our world. But the Stone King requested you—he is the one who ordered you sent to Ulfaria in the first place—and you are rightfully his. Safe travels."

"Fuck you!" I'm yelling at the top of my lungs as the snake starts to withdraw its massive head from the bank of windows, smashing more of the jagged shards of glass around the frame. I'm glad of the cage, otherwise I'd be slashed to ribbons. "SIAN! Fucking *wake up!*"

"She can't hear you," the councilor sneers. "Don't worry. She'll awaken once you're safely away. And she'll have no memory of this event—or any conversation you had before..."

His voice trails down to nothing as the snake spins around and slithers away, with me bouncing in the cold, white-rusted cage around its neck.

It's traveling through the darkness at an incredible speed. The scenery fades into a blur as it shoots along. A distant memory pokes at my mind. Merry...go...round. Ornate, pretty carved horses on long poles, bobbing up and down and spinning around at the same time, going faster and faster... as the scenery in the background faded into an indistinguishable blur.

The adrenaline dump is fading a little, and I'm shivering uncontrollably. But there's nothing I can do right now. The door to the cage was locked securely, and until we get to where we're going, I'm stuck here. So I probe my brain some more, thinking, thinking, straining to recall anything about my past before I woke up in the woods. The merry-go-round memory was vivid, it felt like something I had actually experienced rather than something I was imagining. So I start there, diving back in, squeezing my eyes shut and trying to see the people around me.

Nothing.

Tears soak my cheeks but I don't even have the strength to wipe them off my face. Instead, I shove my hands into the pockets of the tunic, then yank my right one out with a squeal. A drop of blood blooms on my finger. I just cut myself... but on what? Reaching back in with much, much more care, I extract the same kind of bladed snowflake weapon I saw Hunter use to bring down that animal with.

Remembering how he showed me to hold it makes me ache. Carefully, I slide it back into my pocket—the thing is a menace to hold even when I'm not being bounced around in a cage. God knows why it's there, but it gives me little comfort. It's not like I know how to use the thing.

I wish I had paid attention. I wish I had let him show me.

But it's too late now.

This whole situation is just hopeless. And there's absolutely nothing I can do about it.

The Hunter King

The panic reached me too late. By the time Haley's silent call for help vibrated through our soul bond, by the time I flew from the drinking hall to my chambers as if my feet had wings, she was gone.

I take everything in with a single glance: the shattered wall of windows, the toppled furniture, the broken glass—and Sian. She looks dazed.

I growl.

Brokk skids into the room behind me. "What happened?"

The Beta shakes her head, blinking. "I-I don't know."

"Where is she?"

When Sian doesn't reply, I stalk over to her and, taking her by the shoulders, shake her violently. I roar, and the fear is apparent in the Beta's eyes, but her reply is the same.

"I don't remember!"

"Stop it! Let her go!" Brokk's hand on my arm is enough to make me let go of Sian.

A sour, mildewy smell fills the air, crowding out Haley's sweet scent.

"Stone King," I snarl. He has her. I will kill him.

"The Stone King?" Brokk asks.

I nod. I know it in my soul.

"We have no proof. He said he would give us until tomorrow—"

I round on my second-in-command, and Brokk lifts his hands. "He lied."

Sian is rubbing her forehead. "We were here. Talking. Then... no, it's all blank. I feel dizzy." She sits down, heavily, on a chair.

I'm acutely aware of every single dust mote in the air. The whisper of a breeze on my skin. The faraway sounds of night birds chirping. My mate's scent lingers—faint, but I can still taste it on my tongue, like honey. Balling my fists, I let out a groan.

"We'll find her," Brokk says. "He won't harm her if he wants her as—" He stops himself mid-sentence, but it's too late. I've already finished it in my mind.

If he wants her as his mate.

The thought is enough to make me roar.

I'm already at the chest where I store my weapons, slinging a bow over my shoulder and adding various blades to my belt. Fingering an inxi, I have a sudden thought. I tried to teach Haley how to throw one of these—a multi-bladed, palm-sized weapon. She did not enjoy it, and she wasn't able to make the kill when I tried to show her how.

I should have tried harder to connect with her. I should have found the words to explain. *For the love of Ulf, please let her be safe.*

"Your Majesty." Another voice breaks my thoughts.

I turn to see my chief advisor, Mikkan. He's wringing his hands.

"Is everything all r-right?" he stammers.

I growl at him and resume my task, snagging a fur and slinging it over my shoulders. When I rescue my Omega— not if, but *when*—she might be cold.

"The queen is missing," Brokk informs him. "I don't suppose you heard anything?"

"N-no, of course not."

Something in the councilor's tone feels wrong. I glance at him. He's not stroking his beard. Instead, he's squeezing his hands together. He refuses to meet my gaze. He's hiding something. I meet Brokk's eyes and, at his questioning look, give him an almost imperceptible nod.

One of my 'magic' abilities is to send my thoughts to other beings, and sense what they're thinking as well. Usually, I reserve this for wildlife—vines and trees and some animals, like the tyrlee—but if I concentrate, I can do the same with other people. It hurts my head and feels like an invasion of privacy, so I don't do it often.

However, I'm doing it now.

Brokk's eyes widen in understanding. He glances at Mikkan, then back at me, and raises his eyebrows.

I shake my head. *No, don't take him yet. But we will watch him.*

Brokk gives a nod.

Looking around, I'm exasperated to see there's not a servant in sight. I was hoping to summon someone to bring Sian something to drink. She looks terrified. I believe her when she says she does not know what happened. Likely she was bespelled or something. The Stone King uses magic. Rumor has it that's why he looks the way he does— like he's been dead a hundred years—because he cast a spell to prolong his own life. The revulsion is bitter on my tongue.

Once I have gathered together everything I might need, I turn to Brokk. "You leaving?" he asks.

I nod. "Coming?"

He looks to Sian, then back at me. "Yes. Mikkan, ensure Sian is looked after, and given something to drink," he says.

145

"Of course. But may I ask—where are you going?" The worry is etched on the advisor's pale blue face. He's still wringing his hands.

"To rescue the queen," Brokk replies.

I'm in a hurry to leave and even so, I take a moment to study Mikkan's reaction. Just as I thought. He goes even more pale, and I can tell he wants to argue—but what could he say without giving himself away?

I'll deal with him on my return. Right now, Haley comes first.

I will find her, tear the Stone King's face off, and then I'll never let my mate go again.

EIGHTEEN

Haley

FOR HOURS, I ride in the foul-smelling cage, my fingers curled around the bars to help me stay upright. The snake glides first through the forest, then a moonlit desert. I doze on and off, but am exhausted by the time we arrive at our destination: a huge, creepy fortress. Crumbling white stones form a Gothic-style structure with tall, twisted turrets. The snake heads directly for the farthest turret, easily fitting through the gaping, empty hole where a window used to be.

Dust stirs as the snake slithers into a vast, gloomy room. Gray-white mold grows in a film over the stone walls, and flakes from the ceiling. Little beetles scuttle down the walls and disappear into cracks in the floor. The place reeks. I double over, coughing, covering my nose and mouth with my hand.

The snake has come to a stop in the center of the room and is now coiled up, unmoving. Like it's waiting for something. There's nothing here but a bunch of ancient, dusty furniture, a cold, cobbled floor, a few of the same glowing orbs Hunter has in his palace—but not nearly enough to provide any decent kind of light—and, to my horror, a tall, hooded figure standing on a dais in front of a filthy throne.

The figure moves, gliding towards me. Shrinking back in my cage, I press against the slimy bars. Icicles of dread creep up my spine as the huge, shadowy figure approaches until it's standing right in front of me.

"At lassst. My Omega," he hisses, and I bite my lip. My fears have been confirmed. It's the Stone King.

"I'm not *yours*," I say, lifting my chin and staring directly at where I assume his face would be, hidden as it is beneath the shadow of the hood. "I was claimed by the Hunter King."

The Stone King issues more of that weird, wheezy laughter he did last time. "Not to worry. If I find the ssscar of his bite too ugly, I can cut it out." The hood moves back a bit, tilting as if he's looking up, and then I hear him inhale. "You are currently not in essstrus?"

Ew. Instinctively, I cross my legs. "Let me out of here," I say, using the same imperious tone I tried back in Arboron.

"Pity," he continues, "I was looking forward to the rut. No matter. There are potions to induce it." There's a grating noise that hurts my ears as he fiddles with the catch to the door on the cage with his long, sharp-tipped fingers, then the door creaks slowly open.

Now that I could get out, I'm not sure I want to.

"Come now," he says, when he realizes I'm not about to emerge. "You will be treated kindly. You are my new queen."

"I am not," I mutter, but I clamber out of the cage none-theless. At least if I'm out of it, I can run.

"Now go! Make for the Foressst Kingdom and kill any Arborii you find!" The Stone King is addressing the enor-mous snake. He gives a cough. "Essspecially the king."

My blood runs cold. "You can't do that!"

The Slythin turns and slithers to the window. Numb, I watch it until it's vanished. My gut feels like someone poured concrete into it and an icy fist is squeezing my heart. There's a roaring in my ears so it takes a moment for me to hear the hissing wheeze that is the wretched king's laughter.

Please god, I pray as I force myself to face him, *please let Hunter and his people be okay. Please.* Thank fuck he's a good fighter. He conquered the Slythin before. He saved me from one just a short while ago. That one was much smaller, though.

The last time he faced this particular snake, the creature survived—albeit losing a fang.

Jesus. Taking a deep breath, I push those thoughts aside. I can't do anything to help Hunter right now. I have to focus on the stuff I can do.

"Hmmm." The hood is cocked to one side now, and I just know Creepy McFuckface is taking a good, hard look at me. Ew, ew, ew. "Not as slight as I imagined. Not as tiny as the other one. A little more... stout. But pleasing, nonetheless. Your scent makes my rod hard."

Bile rises in my throat, and I swallow it back down. I need to keep my wits about me. Both Sian and Mikkan said that Hunter would never let me go willingly. He might already be on his way to rescue me. And even if he isn't, I have places to go if I get out of here. No, I correct myself firmly, not if, but *when*. On the other hand, if I panic and make Creepy mad, he could hurt me. I need to play along as much as possible until I've gotten my bearings and find a way to escape.

So, when Talons McGross reaches out and caresses the bare part of my thigh, which is easily accessible beneath the hem of the tunic I'm wearing, I clench my fists and force myself to accept his touch. He's assessing me like someone would a horse they had just purchased. A foul scent wafts

149

over me. I want to scream and run away. But right now, all I can do is take it.

It's so different from Hunter's touch—like night and day. I want to shrink into myself, but force myself to stay still.

Will I ever see Hunter again? Feel his hands on my body?

McGross speaks again, interrupting my thoughts. "Such soft flesh. Do all Omegas feel this... sssmooth, I wonder? Diala did, but then..."

"Who?" I sense a way out of this: keep him talking.

"The last Omega queen of Arboron." He gives a little scoff of disdain. "She was a beauty. Until—"

"Until you ruined me," says a female voice. A raggedy pile of blankets in the corner moves, and a hooded figure rises from the filth. A delicate jasmine scent cuts through the mold. "Diala?" I say.

"In the flesh." She sounds tired, but her posture is straight.

"Why are you hiding there?" the Stone King hisses.

"I wasn't hiding. I came here for light. Warmth. This is the only part of the palace you bother to illuminate."

Jesus, I can't imagine how dark the rest of this place must be.

"Watch your tongue," McCreepy snarls. He unfurls his long fingers with the gross nails. Can he do magic like Mikkan could?

I've got to get the fuck out of here.

The Omega queen sways forward, bringing with her the fresh, jasmine scent. Diala is taller than me, but shorter than Sian. While the males here seem to easily top seven feet on average, the females are shorter. This one is the smallest I've seen yet—closer to my size than Sian's. She pulls down her hood. Her skin is a dusky pink, and her hair, markings, and lashes are the deep crimson of a red rose. She's wearing a torn and tattered robe, she's covered in dust and grime, and her hair looks like it hasn't seen a comb in a century, but even so, she's stunningly beautiful.

"You're so young!" I blurt out. "How can that be?" After all, Sian told me that she was wounded and kidnapped by the Stone King decades ago. She doesn't look a day over thirty.

Diala slants her mauve gaze over at Creepy McFuck, and her lips curl at one corner. "Shall I tell her, Your Majesty? How I was wounded when you murdered my mate and came to steal me? How you used magic to suspend me in time until you could find a cure? What happened when you did find a cure, and came to wake me up?" Her voice is cracked, yet still rising. The agony in her is so obvious, my insides twist.

"I should have killed you," the Stone King snarls. "What a pathetic creature you are, ssskulking about in the shadows, always ssscheming... meddling..."

"You should have! Why didn't you?" She lifts her chin.

She's brave as fuck but I'm wincing. She's provoking him on purpose. But why?

"Because you wanted me to," he snaps. "Why reward you, when you fail to give me what I need? Besidesss, I knew I would be procuring an Omega from another planet. I thought she might need... tutelage."

Is he fucking serious? "What is she going to teach me?" I ask before I can stop myself.

"How to be a good Omega. A good queen. Thisss one was much beloved before she fell from grace."

"Fell from grace?" Diala's slim body quivers like a reed in the wind. "You're a monster! A sick, fucking monster!"

More gross, wheezing laughter from the hooded creep. "I admit, I did not intend for my life-prolonging ssspells to have these unintended consequences." He indicates the shadow where his face would be. "But I am still an Alpha. I ssstill have desires. And I can still sssire offspring. All I need is a functioning Omega."

"Never," I say. "I will never submit to you." Moldy dust rains down from the ceiling as my voice bounces off it. "Never be your mate!" So much for staying calm and reasonable.

"Just as there are potions to induce essstrus, there is magic that will make you more... willing," the Stone King says. He seems not to care a bit about my defiance. He's used to being turned down by prospective mates. I slide my hand—very carefully—into my pocket.

"Is there?" Diala asks with an arched brow. She has a point. If there was a potion, he would have used it on her. Once again, I'm struck by her courage. Breathtakingly gorgeous and brave as fuck: she must have been an amazing queen.

"I'm so sorry about your mate," I say, because I'm good at saying the wrong thing at the wrong time.

Her face contorts, and I curse myself for mentioning it. "He was everything to me. Without him, life has no meaning. *Kill me...*" She whispers the last two words so faintly, I'm not sure I heard them.

"What?" I stammer.

She doesn't repeat herself but her eyes, filled with tears and locked on mine, say it all.

There's a deep ache in my heart at the thought that anyone could be so desperate. Then again, when I put myself in her shoes, I can see exactly why she'd want out.

Hell, I'm about to be in those same shoes, and I feel the same way. Only, I don't want to die. I want—

"Enough of this melodrama! Diala, get out of here—or don't, I don't care. I have my new Omega to deal with. Jussst get out of my way." Creepy McFucker's slimy tones interrupt my thoughts. "If you ssstill want me to, I'll deal with you later. I'd be happy to ob—" His words are cut off with an abrupt gurgle. Then there's a cough, and a spray of blackish fluid shoots out from within his hood.

"What did you do?" Diala whispers.

My heart is pounding. What *did* I do?

The tall, hooded figure folds in on himself until he looks like a puddle of robe with two taloned, blue-veined hands sticking out of the sleeves.

"You killed him!" Diala says.

I let out a little huff of disbelief and snatch back my outstretched hand. Diala approaches the puddle and draws the hood back, exposing the creep's head and neck.

The snowflake weapon juts from his throat, right where his Adam's apple would be. Whitish fluid oozes from the wound.

"Did I do that?" My voice sounds like it's coming from far away.

"Yes! I watched you!"

"I can't believe it." I must have reached into my pocket, gripped the weapon without cutting myself to shreds, and then thrown it—accurately—at the Stone King. "How did I do that?"

"Magic?" she suggests.

I choke on a laugh. Maybe I'm better at fighting than I thought.

"You must go." Diala grips my shoulders. "You must get out of here." The walls shake, and beetles and scummy silt rain down.

I dash my hands over my head, brushing filth away. Diala pushes me towards the doorway. There's a distant rumble and the room shudders.

"Get out now while you can," she shouts.

"What about you?" I shout back over the earthquake.

"This whole castle was made by his magic. It will fall with his death."

That's why it stinks in here. "I'm not leaving without you," I say. I grab her arm and pull. Compared to her, I'm surprisingly strong. Or maybe the queen, beautiful and statuesque as she is, isn't in top health. Which makes sense, since she spent decades living with Mr. Gross Snake Mage.

"I cannot," Diala pants as I tow her to the door. "He put a curse upon me, upon this land."

"He's dead." I duck. Another rumble shakes loose a ceiling stone. "You survived, he didn't. But we need to move."

Behind us, the Stone King lies with eyes wide and staring in death. A fuzzy white film has already covered him. *Ashes to ashes, dust to dust. Fungus to fungus.*

I tug Diala forward and push her into the hall beyond. "I need your help to get out."

The stones crack under our feet. Diala sags against a wall. "I cannot. I have never seen beyond these castle walls."

Behind us, the ceiling in the throne room is crashing down.

"I'm not leaving without you," I bellow in her ear. "If you want me to live, you'd better start running."

"Why should I care if you live or die?" she shoots back but she lets me pull her onward. It's not her fault she's in such a bitchy mood. I would be kind of pissy if my husband had died at the hands of our enemy, and the enemy had kept me captive for decades.

The whole hall is rocking. Diala grabs and flings me out of the way before a stone smashes down where I was standing. Bright sunlight flashes down the crack in the roof.

I gesture to it. "There's so much to live for."

"Not for me. You can do this. I can't." But she keeps moving.

Rubble falls onto her dress, pinning her in place, and I help her tug it free. We clamber over mucky stones. Clouds of moldy dust billow out ahead of us.

Diala is now fighting as much for her own survival as I am for mine. When we get to a fork in the hall, she grabs my elbow and guides me to the wall. She presses a worn, square cut stone and a secret door opens up, leading to a tunnel.

"This way." The tunnel is dark but wide enough for us to both fit side by side. Diala has to duck her head. "This leads out of the castle."

"See?" I say. "I couldn't do this without you."

She doesn't answer but when I grab her hand, she grips mine and doesn't let go.

The tunnel air is cleaner than the castle's. The ground still shakes but the smooth earthen walls hold. The mildewy smell dissipates as the cool, clean air flows in. We're heading towards an exit. The tunnel widens, giving us more delicious fresh air. I suck down lungfuls.

We emerge from the tunnel, running hand in hand into the light.

We don't stop until we're well away from the castle. White hot pain runs up and down my legs. My hip is throbbing where the doorway scraped it. Diala has a dark smudge on her forehead, a bruise on her pink skin.

The castle rises behind us, its spires piercing the clouds. Gray smog hangs over the land, turning the sky into a haze, blotting out the suns. My foot hits a stone and Diala keeps me from falling over. We stagger a few more steps, and stop.

I double over.

"What now?" Diala asks.

I hold up an index finger, my lungs too overworked to answer.

The world shakes again and we grab each other to remain upright.

"The Stone King was a magician of great power," Diala mutters. "This is the result of his death curse."

"This planet is so weird."

Diala starts. "You are not from here?"

"Nope. I'm a human from another planet. Long story. Come on!" I find her hand again. Her palm feels familiar after our long escape together. She lets me pull her up the hill, overlooking an endless rocky plain.

A white-gray desert stretches out before us. There's nothing but silt and sand and stones all the way up to the hazy lavender sky. Here and there, boulders break the monotony of sand, along with the occasional twisted, leaf-less tree.

"This place is a wasteland." I scuff at the ground. It's coated with the same whitish-gray flaky stuff that coated the castle walls. "Is this from the spell?"

Diala turns in a circle, her shoulders hunched. "One of them. The Stone King was powerful but his magic required a price. He did not give to the land, he only took. It turned his kingdom into a death-scape."

"This whole kingdom is like this?"

She shrugs.

"What about the people?" I recall the refugees in Hunter's throne room.

"They left, or died."

I wipe my mouth. It's bone dry. I'm filthy, and there's no water. "We need to leave, too."

There's a boom like thunder, and a crack opens up in the desert before us. Diala hustles me back over the crest of the hill. We fling ourselves down into the sand. Behind us, the castle is falling in on itself. Silt rains down. We cover our heads.

"What's happening?" I whisper.

White dust coats Diala's eyelashes. She shakes her head. We both hug the ground, letting the curse-dandruff coat us.

The earthquake fades. A single spire of the castle remains. I rise but Diala yanks me back down.

Over the hill comes a grinding sound, like flint striking flint, magnified a hundred times.

Staying low, Diala and I crawl up the rise. We're coated in the gross dust, so we blend right in with the ground.

That mildewy scent is back. My legs are cramping and my stomach folds in on itself. The sight is so nasty. Saliva pools in my mouth like I'm going to throw up. I swallow my gorge and crane my neck to peer through the rocks we're hiding behind.

The earth has opened up and birthed rows and rows of statues coated in the flaky dust. They're holding spears, and their legs move with a sound like teeth grinding. In the distance, the ground is still shaking, and more statues appear, marching in neat formation. Column after column, as far as the eye can see. There have to be thousands of them.

"I was afraid of this," Diala says in a breathless whisper.

"What is it?" I keep my voice to a barely audible volume.

"It's his army. This is why they called him the Stone King." Diala sounds so sad. I grip her hand but can't take my eyes off the statues. The carving is detailed and surprisingly life-like. A creepy alien version of the First Emperor of China's Terracotta Warriors.

"Do all kings have magic?" I murmur.

"Some more than others. It depends on the land." Dusty creases appear on her forehead. "The Stone King spent every day of his long life building this army and increasing his magic."

And keeping this Omega captive. I squeeze her hand. "How are we going to get out?"

Something sparkles in the corner of Diala's eye. A tear tracks down her dusty face, leaving a pink trail. "We cannot. Soon, the warriors will march, and kill anything that moves. This is the end."

Fuck that. "I'm not dying here."

Diala slants her head down. "You sound like my mate."

The light fades as we huddle together on the hill. What can we do? Sneak back up to the castle? Find a way around it? Sprout wings and fly?

I'm about to share my best idea, which is to crawl slowly back the way we came and regroup on higher ground, when Diala grips my arm.

There's movement in the far off hills. The blast of a horn.

The statues nearest to us remain still. The squadron closest to the hills raise their stone feet and march forward as one, each multiplied step sounding like rocks tumbling in a dryer.

A massive snake slithers over the hill. Its coils gleam pinkish between the gray rocks. Its body is coated with that whitish, waxy substance, but that's flaking off, revealing whole patches of shining crimson scales.

"Slythin," I mutter. This just keeps getting worse. "Okay, if that thing gets any closer, we run back to the castle and find a place to hide." Not the best idea, but it's all I've got.

"What about the stone soldiers?"

"Maybe they'll be distracted by the snake." Come on, I need some good luck now.

"Very well," Diala says. "If we die, we die together."

"That's the spirit," I whisper back. "Your positive attitude is inspiring me."

Her mouth pinches like she's trying to remember how to smile. At least there's some life left in this queen.

The snake ripples over the desert. From our vantage point, it looks like a twisting red ribbon, a banner undulating in the wind. It's almost reached the first regiment, which is marching toward it under a cloud of dust.

"Okay," I mouth, but Diala's staring at the snake.

"Who is that?" she mouths back.

I shade my eyes, not that it helps in such hazy light. The snake's scales are fully red now. The white film has completely rubbed off. There's a dark shape clinging to its neck, just below the snake's wedge head.

"Someone's riding on it." Crap, another soldier type?

"Look." Diala points. Another snake has slithered over the hill. It's bright orange, like a shimmery traffic cone. Huge but not as big as the first red one, the orange snake coasts forward on a tide of what looks like... green moss? A bright grass-colored tide moves ahead of it, rolling down the dusty rocks. Like someone's unrolled AstroTurf over the hills. It's advancing all at once.

"What the..." I forget to whisper. Fortunately, a crack like thunder drowns out my voice.

The crimson snake has reached the first regiment of stone soldiers. The figure on its back raises a black shape and a blast of two notes rings over the desert. Goosebumps rise on my arms.

The snake shimmies over the sand, right up to the stone statues... and it doesn't stop. With a thunk like crashing cars, it smashes its huge coils into the first line of warriors.

Diala and I both choke back gasps.

The snake bowls over another row of the regiment. Stone limbs go flying with resounding clunks. The snake writhes and smashes its way through the formation. Soldiers fall, knocking each other down with a sound like flint striking flint.

The orange snake has reached the foot of the hills. It slithers faster and follows the red leader, bowling over the remaining statues left standing.

Diala and I are standing now. It's safe—the statues nearest us have turned, and the whole army is marching towards the snakes.

But more Slythin are appearing over the green hills. Green and blue, purple and black, shimmering silver and gold—all the colors of the rainbow. The remains of the waxy substance coating them rubs off when they reach the sand.

The head snake is the largest by far. Its colors are as brilliant crimson as a juicy pomegranate seed, glistening against the chalky statues. And a figure is riding upon its back, a green dot on the shining red scales.

"Hunter," I breathe. He's riding the red Slythin, his hips rolling with ease. The slithering creature glides from regiment to regiment, the sinuous coils destroying soldiers with each graceful ripple.

Diala has gone stiff. "Who is that?"

"That's the Hunter King. He's come to save us."

"No," she says, tearing her hand away from mine. "I cannot go."

She takes a few steps, but stops. There's nowhere to run. And she can't stay here.

The remaining troops march out, a foul cloud of dust rising under their stone boots. The horn blasts again and again, and more Slythin appear, turning the hills into a seething rainbow mass. The newcomers swarm over the desert and smother each squadron, leaving no statute standing.

The green tide has also advanced, coating the sand with

moss and grass. Green-branched bushes sprout up here and there. The Slythin leader's crimson folds shimmer against the bright grass.

The orange Slythin has crushed the regiment closest to us. Its coils crunch over the statues like boots tromping on broken pottery. The snake comes slithering forward. Diala whimpers.

"Omega," someone shouts. It's Brokk, riding on the orange Slythin's back.

"I'm here," I shout back.

The snake lowers its head until its jeweled eyes are level with ours. "It is you," Brokk calls, shading his eyes against the bright suns. The haze has lifted off the land. "Are you hurt?"

"I'm okay." Where is Hunter? I want to ask, but the big crimson snake is far away to the left, destroying the statues near the horizon. "What's happening?

"I've never seen anything like it. We came to rescue you. The Slythin accosted us, but he was able to talk to them. He explained they were under the Stone King's curse."

"He explained?" I ask.

Brokk shrugs. "You know him. *Curse. Go*," he grunts in imitation of Hunter. "He told me to get on this big guy." Brokk pets the scaly neck. "He grunted and pointed. So I prayed to Ulf and climbed up. And here we are. The bravest Alphas joined us to defeat the Stone King's army. I don't know how the king knew, but he did."

"And the forest following?" I point to the hills, where trees are sprouting on the edge of what used to be desert.

Brokk cranes his neck back. When he sees the freshly sprouted growth, he jerks in his seat. "Ulfdamn. That isn't a sight you see every day."

"The Forest King's magic," Diala murmurs. "There has not been a record of it in many years."

Brokk's gaze snaps to Diala. His eyes soften, and he puts a hand on his heart. "I have not had the pleasure of meeting you, lady." His voice is a low purr.

Diala sniffs and looks away, but I feel a tremor run through her.

Beyond our vantage point, animated stone statues are attacking the Slythin with their spears. With enough jabs, they could sever a snake's head from its neck. But from what I can tell from the wreckage of most of the regiments, the scaly beasts are winning.

Brokk is still staring at Diala, who's refusing to look at him. The crimson snake's scales glimmer in the corner of my eye.

"Hey, can you help us out?" I ask. "Give one of us a ride?"

"No," Diala gasps, and steps back.

I pull her close. "It's time to go."

"With him?"

"Beggars can't be choosers." I drag her closer to the Slythin. "She'll ride with you."

"I cannot leave you, *majesta*," Brokk says. Diala quakes again.

"Yes, you can." I point to Hunter and the biggest Slythin, who are headed towards us. "My king is about to pick me up."

"Very well. Quickly." Brokk reaches down.

"Go with him." I push Diala forward. "He's nice, I promise." Brokk and I get Diala settled on the snake's neck in front of Brokk. She looks tiny compared to his excessively muscled, Alpha bulk. Or maybe it's just her bowed head that makes her appear so small.

Brokk looks down at her, his fascination obvious.

"I'll see you back at the castle," I say.

Diala lifts her head. Her expression is stricken but her

posture is perfect. She looks like a queen.

She *is* a queen. The Queen of the Forest Kingdom. "Damn," I whisper. I might have just thrown a wrench into the intricate workings of the Arborii government.

I rub my forehead. If Diala wants to rule, she can take over my position. I'm not cut out to be queen.

Hunter rides the red Slythin up to me. This snake is so monstrous, it makes the one that attacked us on our picnic look like a baby. Not only is it missing the white scum on its scales, but no poison is dripping from its fang. Its single fang —this is the same creature who took me here.

I stroll up the hill to greet him and my boots sink into thick moss. The rolling green turf covers the hill, and is advancing towards the castle.

"How is this possible?" I whisper. The answer is a pleasant weight in my chest, a joyful swell in the bond. Hunter is the Forest King. He is truly one with the land.

What does that make me?

I wobble, but a newly grown sapling is there to steady me. I lean on it as Hunter comes closer.

Hunter is in breeches as usual. The muscles of his torso gleam bronze and green in the suns' light.

I lift my arms up to him and he snatches me up, swinging me in front of him and clutching me to his tattooed chest. He steadies me as I sit on the smooth, shiny red scales. His huge thighs squeeze around mine. His musk surrounds me and saliva bursts in my mouth like I've bitten into a juicy fruit. I lean back against his solid frame, dizzy.

The Slythin swerves its sinuous body around and flows towards the hills as the ground rumbles one more time. Behind us, moss now covers the piles of rubble all the way up to the castle. The one remaining tower sinks into the ground. A wind blows over the green plain, and the grasses swish with a hushing sound. Ahead is a grove of trees. The forest has reclaimed this land. The healing has begun.

Hunter digs his fingers into my dusty hair, tugging my face back. His chest rumbles on a growl. "Mine."

I twist around as far as I can, cup his face, and kiss him.

NINETEEN

Haley

BY THE TIME we reach the palace, it is dark. Bonfires burn in every firepit on the lawn. The scent of spiced wine and roast meat hits me and I clutch Hunter as my stomach roars. I need a bath and a meal. Maybe two or three rounds of both.

The bell rings out, and crowds gather on the palace steps. More people throng the fires. The dark shapes of Arborii move out of the way as the Slythin glide right up to the palace.

Brokk rides beside us on his snake beast. Diala sits rigid in front of him, her hands folded tightly in front of her.

"No sign of Mikkan and the others," he calls to Hunter. "I've sent guards to arrest them. We'll announce it to the people, tell them to look out for the traitors."

Hunter grunts.

One of the Stone Kingdom refugees races into our path. Hunter tenses around me, holding me tight as the Slythin rears back, stopping short. It's the same Ulfarri who begged

165

for the Hunter King to help his people. He falls to his knees. "Hunter King, you have saved us."

The crowd breaks out into a cheer. A few of them have gotten their hands on those bellowing horn thingies, and I have to cover my ears. The sound blasts over us. I press back against Hunter.

The people are screaming and crying, raising their hands and bowing. "Hunter King! Hunter King!" they chant.

Hunter squeezes his knees and the Slythin gently curves around the kneeling refugee, heading for the palace steps. More people run onto the lawn once the two Slythin have passed. "Hunter King! The Wild One!"

Hunter's shoulders are rigid. I press my hand into his large thigh. He hates the attention, I know it. His distaste is clear in his stiff body and our bond.

Brokk pulls ahead. His grin is big enough for two Alphas. In his lap, Diala sits with her eyes wide and staring like a hunted rabbit's. This is the first time she has seen her palace in so many years.

"Let me down." I grip Hunter's forearms. "Let me help her." I can relate to an Omega who has no idea what's going on or what's become of her life.

But Brokk slides down and lifts the rigid queen into his arms. "It's all right," he murmurs. "You're safe now."

Diala still looks dazed.

"Haley!" Sian races down the steps. She crosses the lawn and bows. "My queen."

I wriggle until Hunter hands me down, and race to her. I throw my arms around her. "You're safe! Thank god."

There's a yellowish-black lump on her green head but other than that, she looks okay.

"Are you well?" She grips my shoulders, peering into my eyes. "I was so worried! What happened?"

"I'll tell you everything. First... help me." I dust down my filthy tunic. Hunter has dismounted and is looking to me. "I need to help her," I call to him, and turn to follow Brokk, with Sian right beside me.

"Where are we going?" she asks as start running.

"I need to help my friend. She was being kept captive by the Stone King."

"Oh." Sian picks up her pace.

Brokk's up ahead, making a turn down the hall. He's heading to rooms near mine.

"We're going to want food and baths," I say. "But I want to make sure she's settled."

We round a corner. There's no sign of the couple we were following, but Brokk's voice echoes down the hall. I slow my steps and raise a hand to halt Sian. We both creep up to the door, listening to the big Alpha's gentle rumble.

"You'll be all right, lady," he says.

The door is cracked open. I set a hand on it and let it swing open.

Brokk is kneeling in front of Diala as if about to unlace her boots. She's frozen above him, her cheeks ghostly under the white dust.

I clear my throat. "Thank you, Brokk. We'll take it from here."

Brokk rises but bends to take Diala's hand. "You are safe here. I give you my word."

Diala blinks up at him, her hand limp in his. He presses the back of her hand to his brow before lowering it to her knee. With a brief bow to me, he leaves.

Sian and I exchange looks. The big guy looks smitten.

Someone outside the windows whoops, and we all jump. Sian scurries to close the windows. Outside on the lawn, Hunter is standing in the center of a ring of firepits with the largest of the snakes before him. The Slythin's huge wedge head descends. Hunter raises the fang on the necklace he wears and presses it to his forehead, then bows his head as well. Firelight dances, turning Hunter's skin to black, and the snake's scales to flame.

After a moment, the Slythin slithers away, and Hunter stands alone. I clench my hand to keep from clawing at my heart. An ache radiates from the center of my chest. I need to be with Hunter.

But I owe Diala. And she needs me. Hunter doesn't.

"We have another infestation of Slythin," Sian is chattering to Diala. "The Alphas went to hunt them but the king roared at them to stop."

"He did?" I stop short. "He spoke?" Brokk said the same thing, but I still can't believe it.

"I mean, in his way." Sian waves a hand as she sashays back and forth across the room, fetching a water pitcher, glasses, a washing bowl, and a stack of clothes. "There wasn't a lot of explaining, but he ordered them to drop their weapons and stand back. And then the largest snake brought its head down, and the king climbed right on. No one knew what was happening. Brokk was the first to ride, after the king." Sian is still telling the story. "He shouted that the rest of them were cowards, and then a few followed."

Diala is sitting like a statue with her hands in her lap.

"Diala," I say, and she flinches.

I turn to Sian. "Can you arrange for a bath and some new clothes?"

"Done." Sian hurries off, closing the door carefully behind her.

I approach Diala.

"I should not have come here." Her voice is barely audible.

Even though she's slight for an Ulfarri female, I don't

have to kneel to lower my head to be her height. With her sitting stiff and straight and me standing, we're eye to eye. "I know this is hard for you. But this is your home."

"No. Not any longer."

My heart twists. She looks so lost. "Diala, the people will—"

She leaps up, making me yelp. She seizes my forearms, bending to hold my gaze. "You must not tell them. You must not tell them who I am," she says in a strangled whisper. "They cannot know." She looks one second away from throwing herself through the windows to escape.

I gently draw back from her tight grip. Taking her hands, I squeeze them. "Okay. Okay. I won't tell anyone."

"Promise me."

"I promise not to tell anyone who you are. But... won't they recognize you eventually?"

She releases me to cover her face with her hands. "Then I cannot go out. I must stay in here."

There's a rap on the door. Sian is outside.

"What is it?" she whispers when she sees my face. "Is she all right?"

"She says she requires a veil. She's seen many horrors, and is grieving."

Sian's forehead furrows. "Of course. I can have one made right away."

"Omega!" There's a growl from the hall. Hunter is striding towards me with Brokk at his back.

"It's all right," I say to Sian, who's backing away with a small smile on her face.

"Omega," Hunter growls again, and scoops me into his arms.

"I'm fine." I wave to Diala, who's shrunk into the wall by the bathing chamber. I don't want her to think I'm being abducted.

Hunter's scent melds with mine and my mouth is watering for a different reason. He presses his face into my hair as he carries me.

"Hunter," I gasp. "I'm filthy."

"Mine," he growls. Using my hair as a leash, he tugs back my head and kisses me hard.

I hear doors sliding shut. We're in our room, and Hunter is attacking my mouth. His teeth drag over the healed bite mark on my neck, and shudders run through me. My heartbeat pulses between my legs.

"Wait." I am breathless. "I need to get clean. I need this stuff off me."

He carries me to the bathing chamber and sets me down in front of the steaming bath.

"Oh, thank god." I tug at my clothes, impatient to get clean.

Hunter's hands close over the collar of my tunic and he rips it clean off. I help him shuck the pieces away.

We end up face to face. At the darkness in his eyes, my breasts and sex swell. I climb into the tub before I jump him, and start scrubbing. The water turns gray with the silty, flaky mold. Snarled clumps of my hair fall out and float like chalk-colored, many legged spiders. I scrub harder.

Hunter climbs in and stills my frantic movements. The drain gurgles and the disgusting water flows away.

He reaches up, taps a tile, and water cascades down from a hidden spout in the wall.

I stand under the spray and let my head fall back. "This is perfect. Like the waterfall."

Hunter is at my back, running a rough cloth up my spine. I keep my eyes closed as he washes me. I let fresh water run into my mouth as the layers of filth peel off me. Like a Slythin, shedding the film on its scales.

I turn to face Hunter. The water is clear, running between us.

"You were able to speak to the snakes."

He reaches out and presses the tile again, stopping the flow of water. He just looks at me, but I know the answer is yes. The largest Slythin bowed to him on the lawn with the firelight reflecting off its single fang. "But that was the snake you fought—its fang hangs in the throne room. What changed from the first time?"

"Curse," he says, playing with a strand of my wet hair.

"The Stone King put a curse on them?"

Hunter rumbles at the Stone King's name, but nods.

"And when he died, the curse lifted?"

He shrugs.

"You can speak to the Slythin," I say. I reach up to finger the fang on the thong around his neck. Was this Slythin an enemy, or his friend? It seems macabre to wear this but maybe there's a custom here I don't understand. "You saved me. You brought the forest with you. You called it, and it came." I gently let go of the fang and close the distance between us, molding my body to his. "You are an amazing king."

He bows his head and kisses me, lifting me from the bath at the same time. The press of his lips breaks a dam in my sex, unleashing a flood. I lose the moments between the bath and when he lays me down on a thick bed of blankets.

He lets me go long enough to towel me off. I grab his hand, pressing it to my cheek.

"Hurt," he rumbles.

"I'm okay," I whisper.

"Show," he orders.

I lie back, stretching out so he can examine every inch of me. Every mark, every bruise. I tell him of my escape as he follows the path of my story by cataloging each hurt.

Reaching for his cock, he grips the knot. It pulses in his hand, and my inner muscles pulse in echo, clamping down on air. I clench my teeth against the empty agony.

Seed spurts from his fisted cock. It anoints my breasts and splashes over the pointed tips of my nipples. I smear it down my stomach, greedy to taste it, to have it seep into my flesh. My insides quake with the heat and haze of going into estrus.

I am baptized in water, then in Hunter's essence. The curse of the Stone King is gone as if it never was.

"Mine," Hunter growls, and I mouth back the only thing I can.

"Yours."

In the aftermath of our rutting, my body is sore but sated. I lie in Hunter's arms. Our skin is glued together by slick and seed.

Hunter speaks. He lived in the forest, was raised by it. He spoke the language of the forest all along. His source, his strength.

His power is incredible. Compared to his abilities, I've got nothing to offer him as queen.

He traces a finger across my lips. "Sad," he whispers.

"A little." I snuggle closer, laying my hand over the flower-like tattoo on his heart. "I'm glad you saved us. That lady, she's been captive for a long time."

"Omega," he grunts.

A chill runs down my limbs. "How do you know that?" Diala wants to keep her secrets. If she's known to be an Omega, how hard would it be for someone to recognize her as the former queen?

"Scent." Now he's playing with my fingers.

"Is there any way to hide an Omega's scent?" I muse without thinking. "Or reverse being an Omega?"

The sudden dagger of pain in our bond surprises me.

"Not for me," I say. "For her."

The sharpest of the throbbing dissipates, but a tender ache remains. Hunter's face is expressionless, but he's hurting.

"Maybe you can ask the other kings, the ones who have Omegas. Or we can talk to the other humans. I'd love to meet them."

His bronze-flecked eyes are intent as he gazes at me.

"If the magicians can do an Omega serum, maybe they can do a reverse-Omega serum. I wouldn't take it, though." I put a hand to his face, stroking his cheek. "I wouldn't want to."

The emptiness in our bond says he doesn't believe me.

TWENTY

The Hunter King

MY LITTLE LYSIA flower is still asleep when I slide carefully out of bed, tug on some clothing, and go in search of Brokk.

I'm still reeling from my last conversation with Haley. Did she mean it when she said she would remain an Omega if she had the choice?

I'm not so sure.

When she was taken by the Stone King, nothing else mattered but getting her back. Brokk, the other warriors and I were halfway to the Kingdom when I felt the shift. I cannot describe it, exactly, but the ground trembled and the very air changed.

Shortly afterward, we were approached a sea of Slythin led by Nala, the one whose fang I took all those years ago. When I tried to communicate with her, the usual invisible wall was gone and we could understand each other.

My Alphas were poised to attack, but I stopped them.

Using her mind, she told me what happened: she and

her fellow Slythin had been bespelled by the Stone King, and she had been sent personally to take Haley to him.

Brokk stopped me from killing her the moment she admitted this.

Instead, I learned that she had then been sent to kill me, but that somehow the curse had been broken shortly afterwards. She and her brethren were free once again. They had come to warn me. To take me to rescue my mate. Once Nala had finished her tale, she dropped her head in invitation, and I leapt astride her.

Brokk was hesitant to ride Nala's mate, Tax, alongside me, but I didn't give him much choice. Once he had taken the plunge, he in turn mocked the others, who were just as afraid.

Remembering the way he called them cowards, I bite back a smile.

I find him in his chambers, still bleary-eyed. The last couple of days have been hard on everyone.

"Brother," he says, taking the horn from his belt and holding it out.

I shake my head and drop into a nearby chair.

"Come to check on me, have you? I would have thought you'd spend the next several moon-cycles in bed with the queen." He rasps out a chuckle.

I'm growing impatient. I need his help. I just don't know how to ask.

"Council," I tell him. "See Aurus."

"Aurus?" He pushes his braid over his shoulder, thinking. "You want me to organize a council meeting with King Aurus?"

I nod.

"Why?"

"Talk. Queen." Haley wants to meet a fellow Hoo-man. We must decide what to do about the Stone Kingdom, which is now blanketed by a carpet of green. Lush, fertile nature has covered the formerly barren wasteland and is doing what it does best: heal. And maybe we can find a way to help hide Diala. As a fellow Alpha, Brokk may have an inkling about her true identity. But even if he doesn't, he knows she's an Omega. He will want to help her.

"The queen wants a Kings' Council?" Brokk looks skeptical.

I resist the urge to shake him. Instead, I nod.

"I'll get right on it," he says. "Today?"

I nod again.

"And you want everyone there? All the kings?"

I give him a look, and he raises his palms.

"I'm only asking! You don't exactly clarify things," he says.

There's a pang in my chest. Once again, I wonder whether Haley wouldn't be better off with someone like him. Someone who uses words to express what they feel.

Then again, he would never care for her the way I do. Nobody ever could.

There's a pause, during which I can tell he's deciding whether to say something. "Any idea what happened to that Omega?" His tone is deceptively casual.

I shrug.

"Only... I promised I would take care of her." His gaze softens and he stares at a spot in the distance, seeing but unseeing. "She's so beautiful. Don't you think?"

I shrug again. Haley is beautiful. My mate is the most stunning, kind, sweet—

"She carries herself like a queen." His gaze has shifted, and his eyes meet mine. I know he's fishing for information, but refuse to give anything away until I know what Diala herself wants.

After a few long moments, Brokk drops his gaze once again.

"I don't know who she is," he says quietly, "and I don't care. I just have this ulfdamn ache inside me to make her feel safe." He rubs his chest in a gesture I know all too well. I do it often. "It's strange. I feel protective of her. Is that just because she's an Omega, do you think? Or could it be for another reason?"

I lift an eyebrow, bemused by the way color rushes to his cheeks. He's definitely smitten. I can only hope Diala will come to care for him. He would be good to her.

"We need to keep her a secret," he says at length. "There are many Alphas around, all of whom would know her to be an Omega immediately, should they be close enough to scent her. Your Omega is the queen, of course, so they've kept their distance—"

I growl. I can't help it.

"Yes, yes, I know. Sorry." He doesn't seem very apologetic. "It's nature. But..." the color in his cheeks deepens, and he seems to be casting about, working out what to say, "I'm just saying I'm here, if you need help taking care of her. Hiding her. Whatever." He's staring at the floor.

I've never seen Brokk this bashful before, and I chuckle. When he hears it, he looks up and gives me a wry grin.

"Shut up, okay?" he mumbles. "Anyway, I've said my piece. And now, if you don't mind, I have a Kings' Council to organize."

Grunting my thanks, I rise from the chair and clap him on the shoulder. If I could, I would ask him what he thinks about Haley. Whether he believes she's happy here with me. Whether he knows anything about an Omega-reversal serum, or why she would have mentioned it if she didn't want any for herself.

But as always, I cannot find the words, so I remain silent.

Haley

Morning light spills across my face when I open my eyes. The huge bed is filled with pillows and twisting sheets, and no one else.

Hunter is probably out communing with the forest snakes or whatever. Which is fine. He's more comfortable out there than with me. Or maybe he just doesn't like the palace. I get that. The palace isn't my favorite place, either.

But my discomfort is nothing compared to what Diala is going through. I need to help her. Maybe I can get Brokk to send a message to the other kings' magicians, asking about Omega stuff.

It sucks that Hunter took my comments the wrong way. I rub at my chest, trying to dissipate the tension I feel in the bond.

There's a rap at the door. I wrap a fur around myself, and finger a stiff lock of hair. I need to wash. My skin and hair are covered in dried cum. It would be gross if it didn't smell so good. "Come in."

The doors slide open, and Brokk sticks his head in. He keeps his eyes averted. "*Majesta*, I came to tell you to make ready."

I clutch the fur to my chest and slide off the bed. "For what?"

"Today, you travel to the Kings' Council. The king has made it clear that he wants you to come with him."

"Me? Why?"

Brokk lifts his hands in surrender. "I advised against it.

They are going to pester him about the Stone Kingdom. The situation requires finesse and diplomacy and, well..." He grimaces.

He thinks Hunter isn't capable of either of those things. Anger flashes through me. "He did well enough communing with the Slythin," I reply coolly.

Brokk's head snaps up. He blinks at me before jerking his gaze down. "I beg pardon, *majesta*."

"Don't ask me for pardon. Speak more highly of your king. Especially when you are the closest friend he has."

Brokk clears his throat. "The king insists you will be safe with him, and I had to agree. He also wanted me to tell you there's a high chance you will meet another Hoo-man who is also an Omega."

"Oh my god." I nearly drop the fur. "That's awesome. I'll be ready soon. Thank you." I'm going to meet one of the other humans!

I scramble to the bathing chamber. What should I wear to a Kings' Council? What is Hunter wearing?

Where is he, anyway? I should have asked Brokk.

Strange that the summons happened just a few hours after I told Hunter I wanted to meet the humans. Unless... he arranged the Kings' Council. That was why he was gone so early. He went out of his way to help me.

But why didn't he come and tell me himself?

Before I get a fresh tunic, I pause and press a hand to my heart. There's nothing but an echo of pain in the bond.

Haley

My first ride in a flying airship, and I can't even enjoy it. The view is incredible—swathes of desert, snow-capped mountains, a descent into a forest with towering orange trees rising against a lavender sky—but Hunter's tense form beside me keeps me on edge. Or maybe it's that I'm on my way to the Kings' Council, and I have no idea what to expect. Brokk told me what he could, but Hunter hasn't said much. As per usual.

I pick at my nails. I'm in a long tunic and a dark green cloak that's so loose on me, it could be one of Hunter's. Maybe it is. Even though I washed before dressing, I still smell like his seed. The scent soothes me.

Hunter's gaze is on the passing scenery. He's not happy. I don't know how to fix it.

I lick my lips. "Did you arrange this council so I could meet the other humans?" I say to fill the silence.

He grunts. I take that as a yes.

"Thank you." I place a hand on his knee. The tiniest gesture. After a moment, he picks it up in his huge one. We sit holding hands, but my insides have been scooped out. There's nothing in me—no organs, nothing but the emptiness of the bond.

A huge structure has appeared ahead. It's four times as big as the palace in Arboron, with huge golden columns. Golden steps glimmer, leading to a wide road that reflects the light like golden lava. There are golden statues—warriors in golden armor—lining the path to the palace.

The flying ship sets down on the road. The doors open. Before I can rise, Hunter scoops me up. He pulls down my hood, and strides out into the heat.

The statues are real people—big Alphas in armor, holding spears. The air shimmers with the heat of the sun, but the soldiers don't move. Somehow I can feel their eyes on me, and I'm grateful for the hood.

Hunter carries me up the steps, between the columns, through an open door. The ceiling of this place is four stories high. Whole trees grow between the inner columns. Birds chirp above us.

Hunter doesn't put me down until we're at the end of a long columned hall, in a cooler, quieter part of the palace. The walls and doors are brushed gold.

My eyes hurt from the brightness of the palace façade. I blink to adjust them to the cool darkness.

"Someone's decorator sure likes gold," I say.

"You got that right," a voice answers.

Up ahead, a woman pokes her head out of a shadowed door. Her face is small and strange, round with too pale skin. I jolt. I'm looking at another human. I'm so used to looking at Ulfarri, my brain registers her as weird.

"Oh," I huff, pressing a hand over my heart, where the bond pinches me.

"Hello, there," the human says. "It's okay. I'm Kim." She opens the door wider. "Come on in."

TWENTY-ONE

Haley

I STAND in the shadows of the hall, staring at the human. Her face is strange but familiar. She's got short blonde hair, and rounded ears. She's about my height.

Hunter puts a hand to my back and pushes me forward. I step inside the small room and face the other woman.

"Sorry," I gasp. "It's just so—"

"Weird? I know. I haven't seen another human in a while, either. I look pretty pasty white compared to an Ulfarri." She chuckles to herself. Her calm and ease slow my sprinting heart.

The door closes behind me and I jerk around. Hunter hasn't come inside with us.

"It's okay," Kim says. "Your mate will stay nearby. He's not going to go far with you here, that's for sure."

I have to say something. "Really?" I croak. "How do you know?"

"Alphas protect. Betas connect. And Omegas..." She sits and pours a glass of something to drink. "We're supposed to breed. But I have an IUD, so good luck with that, suckah!"

She lounges back on a low couch and stretches out her arm towards the wall with her middle finger raised, as if she's flipping off an invisible person.

I'm still frozen by the door.

"Sit down." She pats the couch. "It's going to take some getting used to me. Might as well be comfortable."

I slowly lower myself onto the couch. "I'm so glad I have a chance to talk to you."

"That's good. I'm told you wanted to meet me as much as I wanted to meet you. Emma wanted to come but she's busy."

"Emma?"

"Another *Hoo-man*." Kim mimics the Ulfarri name for us. "She's pregnant, and you can imagine how protective her Alpha is right now."

"Her Alpha is..."

"Khan. King of Altrim. Emma was the first Omega brought here. The first one to get pregnant, too. The magicians say everything's good and she's healthy, but you know how the Alphas are." Kim waves a hand. "They treat us like pets, not people."

"Oh my gosh, I was just thinking that I felt like an alien trophy wife."

Kim throws her head back, cackling to the ceiling. "Yes, good way to put it. It took me a while to break that mold in my guy's head. But I smashed it pretty good."

I press my lips together. Kim's laugh bounces around the room. She's not pasty at all—her pale skin glows, and her hair has a golden sheen in the low light of the floating orbs. She looks like a queen. An Omega and a human, and comfortable as both while still one hundred percent herself.

I twist my hands in my lap. "They didn't treat their own Ulfarri Omegas any better. I just met one."

Kim scrambles up, coming to her knees. "You met an

Omega? Not a human turned into one, but an OG Omega?"

"Yes." I hesitate, but then explain a bit about the Stone King's magic that extended Diala's life, while leaving out her name or former status as queen. "She doesn't want anyone to know who she is. I wasn't even going to tell Hunter but he figured it out."

"Hunter?" Kim snorts. "Is that the name of the Hunter King?"

"No. He... I just call him that. He doesn't have a name. Or, if he does, he hasn't told me or anyone else what it is." I take a sip of my drink, hoping to hide the bitter twist of my mouth, but Kim tilts her head.

"Trouble in paradise?" she asks lightly.

I shake my head.

Kim barks a laugh. "It's okay. The Big G-A and I got into all sorts of fights when we first got together."

"The Big G-A?" I ask.

"Golden Asshole. That's what I call him. Amongst other things."

I choke on my drink.

"We still fight, actually, but it's a lot more fun." Kim's eyebrows bounce suggestively.

"Oh my god." I set my glass down with a thunk. "Anyway. This Omega I'm trying to help needs a way to hide who she is. Is there a way to hide the Omega scent?"

"Probably, but I'd bet if there is, the magicians frown on it. The way Ulfarri culture is set up, Omegas have so little power. I'm guessing that there are lots of Omegas who'd like to hide their scent and hide who they are. Maybe they're not all extinct, just hiding."

"I just want to help her," I say. "I even asked Hunter if there was a way to reverse being an Omega. Like the Omega serum but the opposite."

"Oh wow," Kim says. "How did Hunter take it?"

"Not well. That might be why he's so upset."

"Probably. It's okay. One good rut will fix it all."

"Yep, that's all I'm good for," I mutter.

"Hey. That's the role they want us to play, but it doesn't have to be that way."

Easy for her to say. "I'm not much of a queen. Or a fighter."

"Wait a damn second." Kim shakes her head. "Didn't you kill the Stone King? Or was that rumor exaggerated?"

For a second I'm back in that stinking castle, staring at a moldy corpse. "No." I shudder. "I did that. I don't know how I did that, but I did."

"How did it happen?" There's a bloodthirsty gleam in Kim's eyes.

"I threw a weapon just right," I tell her. Maybe talking about it will be cathartic. "The thing is, I don't know how. It was a little multi-bladed weapon, like a snowflake."

"An inxi," Kim interjects knowingly.

"Yeah. In any case, Hunter wanted to teach me how to throw that thing properly, but I was too scared to even hold it... until that moment in the Stone King's castle. It was like I had muscle memory that I don't remember building up."

Kim taps her chin. "You could've drawn on his instincts. The Alpha-Omega soul bond is pretty neat that way. I don't remember my Earth life, but I was either a stunt devil badass with a bunch of martial arts training—or the bond worked to give a bunch of Aurus's knowledge to me. Or both. No way to tell, I just enjoy the results."

"You don't remember home?"

She shrugs. "Aurus is home."

An arrow hits my heart. I want to feel that way about Hunter. *Maybe I already do.*

"Do you remember Earth?" I ask.

"A little. I remember some commercials."

"Oh, fun. I remember a few things, but they're fuzzy."

"Emma and I wonder if that's a weird side-effect of the Omega serum they gave us. Amnesia. Maybe the magicians will figure out how to get rid of it, or circumvent it in future." She doesn't seem too concerned either way.

I rub my chest. I need to talk to Hunter. But what will I say?

There's a growl outside the room. It's our only warning before the door bursts open. Kim leaps to her feet, shifting to a fighting stance. But the delicious scent rolls over me, and my limbs relax for the first time since I entered the room.

Hunter is on me before I can speak his name.

I wave to Kim, who's chuckling. "Good catch," she calls and sinks back on the couch, muttering, "I thought *my* guy was big and bad."

I blink at Hunter. He's intimidating as a storm cloud, features twisted into an intent scowl. He's in his usual ready-to-hunt outfit—leather breeches, with a knife tucked into its worn sheath on his belt. His torso is covered in swirling tattoos and scars. His eyes are dark with an emotion I can't pinpoint.

"Where are we going?" I ask, wrapping my fingers around the leather straps criss-crossing his pecs. We're headed down the cavernous hall again, towards a huge set of doors.

Hunter gives me a grunt and nothing else.

"Back to being Mr. Grunty," I say lightly, but inside I'm cold. I guess it's time for the Kings' Council. I should have asked Kim what's going on.

I press my face into the junction of his neck and shoulder, seeking his scent, his warmth. "You're making me nervous, Hunter."

He stops and waits until I lift my head. He runs a finger

along my jaw. "Mine."

Just one word he's repeated so often, but this time I hear its echo in my heart.

The four-story tall doors in front of us glide open. Inside, the ostentatious gold decor is less shiny and more muted. Light spills onto a circular table in the middle of the room. The table has massive King Arthur vibes. A single Alpha sits on the far side, facing the door. Arranged around the rest of the table are empty seats with floating orbs hovering in them. Some glow white, some red. One glows black. Hunter sits down in the only empty space. Beside us is a floating orb that gives off no light at all.

The Alpha at the table is staring at me. Even the orbs seem to be fixated on me, which is ridiculous. It's like I can sense the eyes behind the orbs. They're like the orb the Stone King used to appear in the palace in Arboron.

I shudder, and Hunter tightens his arms around me. I bow my head and let the hood fall over my face. I'm in Hunter's lap, covered in his scent. No one's going to hurt me. He wouldn't let them.

The other Alpha rises, his chair scraping over the floor. He's a big guy with gold armor that matches that of the soldiers we saw outside. "Greetings, Hunter King. I trust you and your Omega are well?"

Hunter just stares at him.

The gold Alpha chuckles, and for a second, his expression looks like Kim's. This must be Aurus, her mate. The G-A.

I allow myself a small smile, hidden by my hood. Clutching Hunter tighter, I probe our bond tentatively, only to be brought up short by the hollow echo in it.

I wish I knew what he was thinking. How he feels about me. Was Kim right? Could Hunter see me as more than just an Omega to rut, the way Aurus now sees her?

It scares me how much I want that.

The Hunter King

"Seems we have had much to discuss," Aurus says, settling himself back in his chair. "Since we last met, the Stone King has met his demise. An altercation involving this very Omega."

Haley is motionless in my arms but the tension is radiating off her. I clutch her tighter to my chest. She's coated in my scent but I'm still glad Aurus is the only other Alpha here. He has a mate so he's not a huge threat to me.

"Thank Ulf." A grunt comes from a white orb. The misty light clears to reveal Khan, the Wanderer King. He leans forward and his long, dark blue hair spills over his shoulders. "No one will miss that creepy fuck."

There are a few murmurs of assent from the kings in the other orbs.

"According to our research," Aurus says, "the Stone King stole the Omega serum from the Ogsul. He paid for magicians to bring Hoo-mans through a portal, and convert them. But the delivery went awry. The magicians panicked, and dumped all the Omegas."

"How many Omegas?" A deep voice, like darkness itself, rasps from the black orb. The Demon King. Haley shudders in my lap and since I can't purr for her here, I stroke her arm.

"No one knows. My warriors are combing the countryside as we speak. There's possibly only one, possibly more. So far, only one has been recovered. And she brought about the Stone King's demise." Aurus swivels his head to me, then his gaze drops to Haley. "How did you manage that?"

There's a slight pause, then she whispers, "Inxi." My chest swells with pride. Even though she was too scared to use that tricky weapon when I tried to teach her, she mastered it when she had to defeat the enemy. Nevertheless, she did kill someone. A king. Will Aurus seek to punish her for that? A protective growl erupts from my throat before I can stop it. My hands tighten on Haley's body.

"No matter." Aurus waves a hand. "His death is ruled just."

I force myself to relax my grip.

"But now we must decide what to do with his kingdom. The land is barren and most of the people are dead, if my reports are correct." Aurus keeps his gaze fixed on me. "Perhaps the King of the Forest can confirm?"

I remain quiet. The silence stretches on. I wish I could find the words. This is as awkward as the public audience in the throne room where the refugees asked for help. Except here there's not even Brokk to help answer questions. And no councilors who turn out to be ulfdamn backstabbers.

Every muscle in my body is rigid as rock. I hate this. But I must do it for my kingdom. For Haley. My little lysia flower.

Aurus sighs. "My reports tell me a forest has appeared where there once was desert. If this is true, then it could be seen as an invasion of the Stone Kingdom by the Forest Kingdom. So, Hunter King... if you wish to correct this conclusion, now is the time to speak."

How do I tell him my intentions? I want to roar with frustration. Haley is vibrating against me. I look down to see her tugging her hood back to reveal her exquisite face.

Her stunning dark eyes meet mine, and warmth floods my chest. She presses her little hand to my skin, covering the lysia tattoo with her palm.

We share a quiet connection, a deep knowing. She understands me. We just don't communicate with words.

Gradually, she stops vibrating against me. *Calm, my little flower,* I urge her silently.

She turns and clears her throat. "I speak for the Hunter King." Her high-pitched voice echoes off the golden walls. I ache with pride.

"We do not allow Omegas to speak at the King's Council," Aurus says.

She rears up in my lap. "Have you told this to Kim? I'm sure she'd be interested to hear that."

Aurus's mouth snaps shut. I bite back a smile.

She settles back against me. "I am the queen of Arboron. At this time, the forest has spilled over into the Stone Kingdom, but we have no wish to annex their borders. The land is barren, and at this point, we are merely providing aid to the people who have suffered under the Stone King's rule for so long."

"Omega—" Aurus begins tersely.

"Let her speak," Khan says, folding his arms over his chest. "This is the most I've heard from the Forest Kingdom in a while." He shoots me a pointed glare, and I bristle.

Then another wave of Haley's sweet honey scent tinged with my musk reaches my nostrils, soothing me. The last time Khan and I met, he was clutching his tiny pink Omega in his arms. Now the roles are reversed, only instead of having to protect my mate from several Alpha kings in the room, I must deal with only one. And he has a mate. I have a newfound respect for Khan. Everything changes when you discover the soul bond.

My focus returns to the Hoo-man in my lap who is proving with every word why she is perfect in every way. Perfect for Arboron. Perfect for me.

"Like I said, the Arborii people wish to aid their neighbor," Haley continues. "Arboron will support the Stone Kingdom. Just until the Stone Kingdom is restored."

"Then who will be king?" Aurus asks.

"We will have them vote on it."

"A vote?" Aurus echoes.

"Yes." She takes a breath. "Each refugee camp or village will elect their own leader. In the meantime, we'll have an interim ruler who helps guide the kingdom to stability. The Forest Kingdom stands ready and able to aid wherever necessary."

Unable to give voice to my pride, I squeeze her knee.

"And how do we know Arboron will not annex its neighbor?" Khan asks.

"There will be a time limit on how long the interim king can rule, and then there will be a kingdom-wide vote. Every adult member of the Stone Kingdom will say who they wish to be their king. No Alpha is allowed to do violence, and no Beta is allowed to do magic to influence the outcome." Haley's voice is sweet, and clear as a bell.

"We can speak with the Stone Kingdom's magicians to see how they would suggest setting up the vote, and how to make it fair and equitable for every adult citizen," Khan says slowly. "Omegas included," he adds with what looks like a wink in Haley's direction.

He is on our side, yet I still clutch her possessively to my chest. She is mine.

Mine.

"There are no Omegas," intones a deep voice from the black orb. The Demon King.

"Excuse me." As well as outrage, there's a squeak in Haley's voice. The Demon King unsettles her. Then again, he unsettles everybody. "There are at *least* three."

"And perhaps soon to be more," Aurus says. "My magicians tell me a great magic was unleashed at the last full moons. The Stone King brought one Omega through the portal with his stolen magic. Perhaps there were others."

The orbs around the table seem to glow brighter.

"Is anyone against the proposed plan to rehabilitate the Stone Kingdom?" Aurus makes a show of looking this way and that. When no one speaks up, he asks, "What about you, Hunter King? Does your queen speak for you?"

There's a pause. I splay my hand over Haley's flat stomach. "Yes," I say.

"Then we will wait for your word to see whom you install as interim king." Aurus rises from his seat. "The Kings' Council is adjourned."

Still cradling Haley, I rise and head to the door, bursting through it.

In the hall beyond, there's a small crowd of gray-hooded Betas and armor-clad soldiers. They all scramble out of the way.

"Mine," I say, kissing the top of my little flower's head.

"Yes, I know." She leans up and presses her lips to mine. Her taste on my tongue is like nectar. "Now take me home."

Some would say that Omegas should be meek and docile, quiet and submissive. Like Diala. But what Haley just did for me in that council meeting—she can find the words when I cannot. And unlike my so-called advisors, she is on my side. Completely.

As we head back to our transport, I marvel at how my little lysia flower has changed my life. Changed me. I feel a connection, a belonging that was never there before.

She is perfect for me in ways I couldn't even imagine, giving me things I didn't even know I needed.

Haley completes me.

TWENTY-TWO

Haley

THERE'S a crowd on the palace steps when our flying ship glides down. The bell rings out to greet us.

Sian waves to us from the top step. A slight figure stands beside her wearing a veil and heavy robes despite the warmth of the late day suns.

Brokk pushes through a group of Alpha guards. "How did it go?" he demands.

"It went great," I say.

"Really?" Brokk squints at Hunter. I'm going to enjoy informing him of his new role. Hunter and I talked it out on the ship. Well, I talked and he listened, and when I felt his warmth and contentment in the bond, I knew our plan was solid.

"That's right. I spoke for Arboron—as queen."

"You?" a courtier gasps.

"Yep. Me. Omegas are people too."

On the top step, Sian is nodding and grinning.

Brokk strokes his beard. "What did you say?"

"I told them our plans for the Stone Kingdom. They agreed to them. We're appointing an interim king for a temporary period, until the kingdom is stable."

"Who?" Brokk asks.

"You," I retort. I lean back against Hunter, who's a solid wall behind me. I grin at the shocked look on Brokk's face. "You're going to handle it. First, you're going to handle this week's palace audience, and answer everyone's concerns."

"What?" a few councilors exclaim along with Brokk.

"You can handle it." I say. "The king trusts you. You'll probably end up retelling your role in the glorious battle with the Slythin."

Brokk keeps opening and closing his mouth, but no sound is coming out.

"Do a good job, because after this, we're sending you to the Stone Kingdom for a while, along with some rebuilding supplies and a team of your choosing." I grin up at him. "You're gonna be the interim king."

Hunter slaps Brokk's shoulder.

The Alpha looks dazed. "What?"

"The Forest Kingdom will give you as much aid as you need," I say loudly enough for all to hear. "We will send you with resources and provide regular shipments until the Stone Kingdom has been rebuilt. This is an interim position but you have the king's trust. And mine."

Hunter slaps Brokk's shoulder again, harder this time. It seems to jolt Brokk out of his stupor and he does the only thing he can do.

"I am honored, my queen." He steps back and bows with a hand over his heart.

"You'll do a great job. And don't worry, we'll be fine without you. I'm going to help with the royal audiences. As for the Stone Kingdom, we'll set up a vote so the people can choose their own leader when your temporary rule is over. I'll explain how it all works."

"What's a vote?"

I wave a hand. "We'll ride that snake when we come to it."

Someone's pushing through the crowd, a small figure in an opaque gray veil, accompanied by a subtle jasmine scent. "I wish to go with him," Diala says quietly.

"Very well," I say. There's less of a chance of people recognizing her in the Stone Kingdom. "Brokk will need all the aid he can get." And this is the perfect solution, until we can find a way to disguise Diala further.

"My king?" An Arborii steps forward. "Is this your wish?"

"I speak for the king," I say. Hunter just glares at everybody until the courtier backs away.

I turn to him and press close. "Take me home." He grunts and scoops me up. He strides through the parting crowd to the palace but I squeeze his arm to gain his attention.

"Not the palace," I say. "*Our* home."

His lips curve up into a smile.

Haley

The scent of herbs is thick on the night air when Hunter carries me up to the waterfall. The cool mist hits my face, and I'm home.

The glowing orbs flicker on as we enter the cave. The place is just as we left it. Maybe he has little elves or fairies or tiny Slythin come through and clean when he's not here.

Hunter crouches to light a fire in the brazier. On our way here, we stopped by the river and, in the light of the moons, we fished. He taught me to kick over a rock and spear the little critters with a dagger. The fish are purple with lots of crazy little dangly things hanging off them. Hunter will know how to cook them and make them smell delicious.

I occupy myself with shaking out the furs and rearranging them into a nice, silky pile while Hunter builds the fire. When he's done, the crackling flames make shadows flicker on the walls. I'm still fussing with the rounded bed I've made with the furs—I just need a few cushions from the palace, and it will be perfect—when I sense him looming behind me.

"I can't believe you knew how to speak with the snakes all along," I say without turning around. My hands itch to position a fur just so. I lean over and twitch the shiny pelt into place. "You have so many powers that I'm just discovering."

He slips a hand around me, pulling me back against him. Heat pools in my belly. The bed I made for us is ready, and so am I. But first, I turn and grip his shoulders. "Not yet. First, I have to tell you something."

His face gets that blank look that means he's worried. I pull him down on the furs and face him.

"You were with me, when I was in the Stone King's castle," I say. "Our bond was strong. That's how I was able to kill him."

He grunts, angling his head away.

"I'm not upset. I'm happy." I scoot closer. "I want to be with you, but I need to tell you this, first." I bite my lip a moment, raising my face so my tears spill out and slide down my cheeks. Hunter looks so worried, but I am happy. "I don't need you to know your name," I tell him. "I don't need you to talk, or explain to me. Your actions and our bond tell me who you are." I cup his beautiful face in my hands. "You don't have to speak, if you don't want to. I can speak, and we are one. Any time you wish, I can speak for you."

He presses his forehead against mine, rocking back and forth. In the bond between us, the ache is gone.

"Name," he grunts. He places my hand on his chest. "Mine."

"You know it?"

He gives a nod. His eyes are gleaming in the low light, the specks of bronze look golden.

"You can tell me," I whisper. "But even if you don't, I love you."

Hunter's sigh creaks through him. He presses me back on the furs. His lips meet mine, plundering. I surge up and plunder right back. I claw at his back, fighting to get closer to him. He pins me down and angles his leg so his knee rubs the seam of my legs. The movement catches my clit through the tunic. Pleasure ripples through me, and a waterfall of euphoria surges into our connection. I gasp, and he breaks the kiss.

His lips brush my ear.

"Torren."

Thank you for reading Haley & Torren's book!

For more news about the series, download this short freebie starring more of Kim & Aurus. You'll be on a special email list where you can

be the first to hear about what's next in the series.

Let us know if you want Diala & Brokk's story!

And if you fancy the Beast King, you can preorder it HERE!

WANT MORE PLANET OF KINGS?

Brutal Mate - Emma and Khan's story

Brutal Claim - Kim and Aurus's story

Brutal Capture - Haley and the Hunter King

Brutal Beast - Rose and the Beast King

A Gift for the Alpha - very short bonus novella starring Kim and Aurus with cameos of Emma and Khan

You can sign up to receive the story for free HERE: http://geni.us/Alphagift.us/Alphagift

LEE SAVINO

Lee Savino is a USA today bestselling author of smexy romance. Smexy, as in "smart and sexy." Find her in the Goddess Group on facebook and download a free book at www.leesavino.com!

Find her at:
www.leesavino.com

Want more growly alphas? Check out the Berserker Saga. Start with Sold to the Berserkers.

Remember to download your free book at www. leesavino.com

The Berserker Saga

Sold to the Berserkers – Brenna, Samuel & Daegan
Mated to the Berserkers - – Brenna, Samuel & Daegan
Bred by the Berserkers (FREE novella only available at www.leesavino.com) - – Brenna, Samuel & Daegan
Taken by the Berserkers – Sabine, Ragnvald & Maddox
Given to the Berserkers – Muriel and her mates
Claimed by the Berserkers – Fleur and her mates

Ménage Sci Fi Romance

Draekons (Dragons in Exile) with Lili Zander (ménage alien dragons)

Crashed spaceship. Prison planet. Two big, hulking, bronzed aliens who turn into dragons. The best part? The dragons insist I'm their mate.

Paranormal romance

Bad Boy Alphas with Renee Rose (bad boy werewolves)
Never ever date a werewolf.

Possessive Warrior Sci fi romance

Draekon Rebel Force with Lili Zander
Start with Draekon Warrior

Tsenturion Warriors with Golden Angel
Start with Alien Captive

Contemporary Romance

Royal Bad Boy
I'm not falling in love with my arrogant, annoying, sex god boss. Nope. No way.

Royally Fake Fiancé
The Duke of New Arcadia has an image problem only a fiancé can fix. And I'm the lucky lady he's chosen to play Cinderella.

Beauty & The Lumberjacks
After this logging season, I'm giving up sex. For...reasons.

Her Marine Daddy
My hot Marine hero wants me to call him daddy...

Her Dueling Daddies
Two daddies are better than one.

Innocence: dark mafia romance with Stasia Black
I'm the king of the criminal underworld. I always get what I want. And she is my obsession.

Beauty's Beast: a dark romance with Stasia Black
Years ago, Daphne's father stole from me. Now it's time for her to pay her family's debt...with her body.

TABITHA BLACK

USA Today bestselling author Tabitha Black loves to write steamy books featuring growly, dominant Alphas and the women who love them. Her latest forays are into dark paranormal romance, including the deliciously hot world of M/f Omegaverse.

She has a weakness for great coffee, strong, dominant men, and tattoos.

Tabitha loves getting mail, so if you want to drop her a line, please do so at tabitha_black@hotmail.com. You can also sign up for her newsletter, follow her on BookBub, or join her Facebook page. Thank you for reading!

Don't miss these other exciting books by Tabitha Black!

Contemporary

His Empire Series
Restraint - Book 1
Denial - Book 2
Anticipation - Novella

Masters of the Castle Series
Fulfilling Her Fantasy
Sharing Silver
Tempting Tasha
Undoing Una

Midnight Doms
Her Vampire Addiction

Anthologies
When the Gavel Falls (Sharing Silver)
Witness Protection Program (Tempting Tasha)
Dominating His Valentine (Anticipation)
Daddies of the Castle (Undoing Una)

Paranormal

Alphas of Sandor
Primal Possession - Book 1
Primal Mate - Book 2

Planet of Kings - With Lee Savino
Brutal Mate - Book 1
Brutal Claim - Book 2
Brutal Capture - Book 3
Brutal Beast - Book 4

Audiobooks
Little Tudor Rose
Conquering Cassia
Restraint
Sapphire's Surrender
Primal Possession

Made in the USA
Las Vegas, NV
11 April 2022

47293092R00115